FATALITIES OF THE MODERN

THE COMPLETE COLLECTION

LENA MA

CONTENTS

Fatalities of the Modern:
The Complete Collection

Lena Ma

Copyright © 2021

Cover Design by EmCat Designs

LASACTKA
THE END OF HUMAN INTELLIGENCE

Fatalities of the Modern World Book One

CHAPTER 1
THE DESTRUCTIVE AFTERMATH

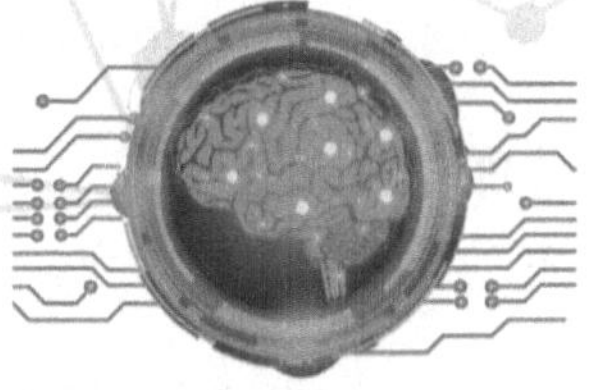

Year 2086

"Who ordered the hot caramel maki-a-ah-o… the caramel thing!?" the barista excitedly hollers.

The café is dingy and dark, the overhead lights flickering. Most of the lighting is provided by the blazing sun streaming through the cracks of the windows.

Still, it only aids in highlighting the adhesive spots on the soiled floor.

"Um… I think I did?"

A young woman, dressed in maroon overalls, chestnut brown boots, and a dark grey beret, quietly answers, approaching the counter while violently whacking her phone against the palm of her hand in attempts to get it to turn on.

"Okay, what's your name?" the barista asks the woman.

"Um… I forget."

"Miss, are you okay?" the barista probes again.

"I don't know. I think so. Maybe?" The woman blankly stares at a deep groove in the counter, her eyes glazing over. "I'm not quite sure."

"Can I call anyone for you?" The barista eyes the phone the woman is desperately trying to turn on. "Maybe a family member or a friend?"

"I don't remember if I have any." The woman glances around the café. "Where am I?"

"Inside a café, miss. Welcome to Baxxes! Are you sure you're okay?"

"Um… no? Do I like cara… cara… carameeel?" the young woman questions, distracted from their previous conversation.

"I don't know. Do I?" the barista inquires back, unaware of whom the question was directed toward.

"Hmmm… well, if I like it, then you must like it too, right?" the woman confidently answers, taking a sip.

Her eyes widen. "This is the BEST thing I've ever tasted! It tastes like candy! Except, you know, it has water in it. It tastes like candy with water in it! Here, try some!"

She exclaims as she thrusts the cup out toward the barista.

"Really? Candy with water!? No way! I've never heard of such thing before! Give me! Give me! Let me try!"

The enthusiastic barista snatches the cup of caramel macchiato and chugs it.

She hastily spits out the contents within seconds.

"HOT!!! IT'S SO HOT!!! AHHHHHH!!!!"

She painfully screams while running her burnt tongue beneath the faucet.

Moments later, the barista turns around and loudly interrogates the young woman. "WHY IS IT SOOOO HOT!?!?!"

The woman, still fascinated and puzzled with getting her phone to turn on, responds, "I think maybe the sun is too hot today so it shines its heat onto the cup, making it hot as well. Maybe it'll be colder tomorrow when the clouds come out. I think it's supposed to rain tomorrow. My dog told me so.

My dog is always right. I love him so much! His name is Mooch, and I would love to show you a picture of him, you know, of him wearing a bumblebee costume last Christmas, but my stupid phone won't turn on. Hey, you have a job! You're smart, right? How do I get this stupid thing to turn on?" The woman forcefully demands as she shoves her phone onto the marble counter in front of the barista.

After minutes of attempting to cool her scorching tongue, the barista takes a look at the young woman's phone. She becomes captivated by the colors of her case as the glitter flowers sparkle beneath the dusty lighting inside the quaint café. She has never seen a contraption this mesmerizing before, and she cannot help but explore every crevice of the phone.

The barista takes her right hand and aggressively strikes the face of the phone a few times, unable to turn it on. She places it under hot water from the faucet since that had loosened her pickle jar earlier, believing the faucet is the answer to everything. Still, no luck.

She then places the phone on the grill, the same grill used to make paninis and flatbreads for the customers, and she attempts to cook the phone on. Nothing.

"Sorry, I think it's broken," the barista shouts as she waves the phone at the young woman.

However, the woman pays no attention to the barista. She is too busy checking out the brooding man across the room, wondering if she could ever look like him. She quickly snaps a picture of him with her disposable camera, throwing it in the trash immediately after as she could never figure out how to get her photos from such a miniscule device.

"Excuse me, ma'am. EXCUSE ME! LISTEN TO ME!" The barista deafeningly repeats. "This is broken. BROKEN!" she squawks as she hands the phone back to the woman.

Without looking up, the young woman waves her hand at the barista. "Oh, just throw it in the trash then. I'll just get another one. All my phones keep breaking. I take a selfie. I lose a phone. I take a selfie. I lose a phone. This keeps happening! Do you know what I mean?"

"Oh yeah, totally!" the barista heartedly agrees. "It happens to me all the time too! That's why I need this job, so I can keep paying for them!"

"I wish there is a button or a key that can just turn on these stupid phones. That would be AMAZING! No, wait! I wish there is a store that sells phones that never break! I should invent one!"

The woman ignorantly declares as she clutches a half-empty iced matcha latte off the table beside her with the name "Logan" written on the side of the cup. "I believe this is mine," she says to the man at the table and walks out.

"Sounds like a fantastic idea! Keep me posted! You can find all my contact information, including my address and credit card number, on my Selfiegram page. I always keep them updated in case anyone needs to find me," the barista bellows behind the woman. "Mocha fra… fra… frapa… frapee… frapee… Who ordered the snow-temperature mocha frapeekeeno!??"

Meanwhile, inside a well-renowned and prestigious medical school…

A cadaver lies open on a steel table. Students are seated behind their desks, copying down a sketch of the human brain from the whiteboard in front of them. Their professor,

Dr. Mullesk, paces back and forth, occasionally prodding the corpse with his pencil as he strides.

"Class, who can tell me the mechanism by which a virus latches onto the neural receptors in the brain and prevents the release of the neuron ball-shaped things? Yes, Sarah?" Dr. Mullesk probes.

"Oh, I forget," Sarah responds as she slowly lowers her raised hand.

"Okay, does anyone else know the answer? Yes, Barrett?"

"I'm sorry, what's the question again?" Barrett asks.

"The mechanism of… the mechanism of… of… Hold on, let me look it up again," Dr. Mullesk replies as he rummages through his textbook once more. "Shoot, now I can't find it. Alright, class, you can all go home. NO SCHOOL!"

Across the street from the medical school…

Sirens blare, lights flashing blue and red against the passing cars as a portly police officer walks over to the offender's vehicle. He keeps one hand hovering over his gun as the window of the automobile rolls down.

"Sir, do you know how fast you were going?" the officer interrogates.

"Really, really fast! LIKE A RACE CAR! I want to be a race car driver when I grow up!" the 50-year-old man inside the SUV exclaims.

"Really? Well, then, I think you need to go even faster if you want to win! Good luck!" the police officer cheers on the offender, walking away and letting the man go.

Behind the scene, a woman is holding onto her toddler's hand and begins to cross a busy street…

"Lauren, you are receiving an incoming call from your mother. Do you wish to accept?" the automated voice receptor of the woman's phone announces.

Lauren stops in the middle of the crowded street to answer her phone, unaware that the light has changed and cars are beginning to speed toward her. Her toddler pulls urgently on her skirt, itching to finish crossing, but Lauren pushes the small hand away and pulls her purple velvet skirt back up as she raises her phone to her ear.

"Hello?" Lauren answers. "Yes, this is Lauren. Who is this? Actually, who's Lauren again?"

"Hey! Watch where you're going, you stupid bitch!" one of the drivers screams, heavily drunk, failing to steer away from Lauren and her toddler.

A crackling crunch is heard as the colliding bodies crush against the front of the vehicle. The blunt momentum sends them flying, blood spilling across the pavement.

Glass shatters as the bodies break through the front window of the café. Not a single person inside the café looks up, and instead, continues to sip their cappuccinos as if nothing has happened. The stares of the patrons are slack, and slobber drips from the mouth of one woman sitting by the back door.

Outside, the siren stops blaring. The police officer, becoming one with those inside the café, steps over the limp bodies as he enters Baxxes and sits at a table.

"Hey! Watch where you're flying!" the barista yells as she finds the mess of glass shards and corpses on her floor. "I just cleaned that!"

Blood pours from the flaccid bodies. Person after person enters the picturesque café, stepping over the corpses without saying a word, even as the blood stains their shoes.

The patrons of the café remain silent, carrying on with their daily routines as if nothing unusual around them is happening.

CHAPTER 2
THE INFECTION BEGINS

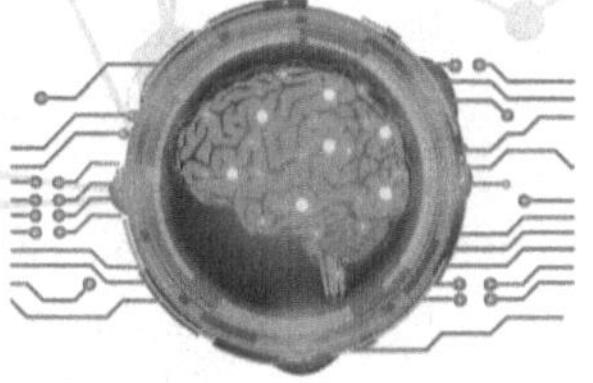

Year 2085

"LADIES AND GENTLEMEN, welcome to the 50th anniversary of the Synapselligence Awards. As many of you know, the Synapselligence Award is bestowed every year to the scientist who has successfully proven the greatest breakthrough among scientific history. These awards are only presented to the very best, the rare few who have proven their capability and intelligence in changing the face of the Earth.

This year, the Synapselligence Society of Scientific Significance would like to grant the award to Samantha Mare for her groundbreaking creation of 'Lasactka', a novel virus proven to increase the intelligence quotients of all human beings to 200, generating a knowledgeable and civilized society where we can become capable of conquering all feats. Let's welcome Samantha Mare!"

The vast audience of scientists, researchers, professors, and physicians enviously clapped as Samantha gracefully walked onto the stage. She was dressed in a sleek silver gown with matching heels and dangling platinum diamond earrings.

Samantha Mare was a beautiful woman, her skin glowing under the light as her long brown waves brushed through the air. Although physical stunning, Samantha was also intellectual, independent, and resilient, and many scientists found her intimidating.

Her unique mind allowed her to think of unimaginable creations and inventions, causing her colleagues to both praise her and become covetous of her.

She held her head high as she strode among her colleagues. Not a single person in the room had achieved what she had, and none ever would, not without her help at least.

Boldly standing tall, Samantha knew she had changed the face of society. It was time others came to terms with what that really meant. For better or worse, they would all be equals in the truest sense of the word.

"Thank you, Chris. Thank you so much. I'm so honored and grateful to be given this year's Synapselligence Award. The Lasactka virus has been my primary research focus for the past five years, starting from when I worked as a post-doctoral fellow at the underground laboratory of Hygoltz in the heart of the Himalayas with the well-known and loved, Dr. Farrow.

The Lasactka virus is a hydrophilic organism that thrives

on the fluids inside our brains. It travels from neuron to neuron via mechanism by the synapses, multiplying, until it spreads out and is collected and released with the neurotransmitters into the rest of our bodies.

The Lasactka virus alters the way our bodies interact with our brains, providing us with great strength and balance as our two conflicting parts merge into one being. This physical and mental balance channels our energies within and allows us to reach deep inside ourselves and unleash the knowledge we already possess but fail to use.

We are a society of great potential. However, we only utilize a fraction of our brains throughout our entire lifetimes while failing to see that we are capable of using much more. We allow our insecurities to prevent us from channeling our inner intelligence.

We see others as more intellectual because of their higher IQs, and we hold back while assuming others will carry on the success of our union.

But look around you! Our civilization is deteriorating with each passing day. Technology is crashing. Computers are leaking personal data because our privacy systems have been built with half a brain. Our medical devices are only doing what is 'just enough' to prevent death without seeking to promote greater health, and even then, patients are still dying. Automobiles have been faltering for the past seven years because we still follow blueprints from 30 years ago.

We look at our children and each other, and we wonder why and how some of us are smarter than others. We're not! We only think we are because some of us harness more of our own inner energies than others, therefore, giving us more confidence to channel the aptitude that lies within all of us.

Not anymore! Last week, Lasactka was released into the general public, latching onto the systems of each and every one of you this very minute. Within days, you will begin to feel your energies change.

You will begin to feel lighter and more capable of performing incredible tasks. With Lasactka, all your energy will be channeled to full potential. We will all be forced to use 100% of our intelligence, making us a society of great power, where we can overcome all dangers and build the greatest civilization known to mankind!" The crowd applauded and cheered as Samantha finished her speech.

"Thank you, Samantha. Let me be the first one to say, I truly admire your work. I have definitely felt a difference ever since Lasactka was…" Chris suddenly froze, his words slurring as his mouth drooped to one side.

His focus faded from his eyes as Samantha waved a hand in front of his face.

"Chris? Chris? Are you alright?" Samantha questioned, concerned.

"Duh… uh… what was I saying again?" Chris asked.

"You were saying how you felt different after Lasactka was released into the public," Samantha reminded him.

"Duh… yeah… oh yeah… I is good!" Chris exclaimed as he held his thumbs up.

"Chris! What is going on with you? Why are you acting strange?! I'm sorry, ladies and gentlemen, Chris seems to have had a concussion of some sort." Samantha turned toward the crowd and apologized.

She turned back to Chris and slapped him across the face.

"Chris! Snap out of it! What's going on with you!? Answer me!"

Without a thought, Chris doubled over in a fit of uncontrollable laughter. Samantha grabbed his shoulders, trying to pull him upright, but he continued to laugh and brushed her off.

Samantha stepped back, stumbling in her heels as she looked out into the crowd. Dozens of faces blankly stared back at her, mouths slightly ajar and comprehension gone from their expressions.

Their faces seemed slack, as if the muscles in them stopped moving all at once, and they began to mumble a strange combination of words and sounds. Samantha's hands shook as she backed away toward the curtain behind stage, head piercing from the overlapping murmurs.

"What?"

"Where am I?"

"This isn't home, is it?"

"Excuse me! Is this my house?" one of the women shouted to Samantha. "It doesn't look like it, but I could be wrong!"

"Excuse me! Do you know the password to unlock my phone!? I think it's my birthday, but I can't remember my birthday!" a man in the crowd asked those around him.

The crowd continued to become distorted and confused, trampling over each other as they all headed toward opposing doors in attempts to find the exit.

"What the hell is going on?" Samantha questioned to herself as she stared out into the confused crowd. "Why is everyone acting... well... stupid? Can it be? No, it can't be Lasactka. I perfected it. It's flawless. This can't be it! Can it?"

Fearful as to what she may have just started, Samantha kicked off her heels and scooped up the skirt of her dress. She then ran toward the back exit behind stage. No way could she escape through the front entrance; the swarms of people were tripping over and running into each other.

She needed to get home and out of the spotlight. Nobody could know she theoretically caused this. Nobody could ever know. She ran along the sidewalk, dodging and stumbling over people as she went.

The stones and pebbles on the asphalt were sharp against the soles of her feet as she made a last-minute decision at a fork in the road. She turned left toward her lab instead of going home. She had to find out what had gone wrong, why her virus had done the exact opposite of what it was designed to do.

Along the way, she began to see more chaos caused by the stupidity everyone around her seemed to possess.

"No! No! No!!! Not my car!" Samantha screamed as she watched two other cars collide into hers because the drivers had forgotten how to brake. "Fuck it. I'll run!"

As she continued to scurry, she heard people around her stopping arguments midway as they had forgotten what they were arguing about. She spotted other individuals drinking from puddles caused by the aftermath of the rain.

Samantha slowed and halted as a car screeched toward her, hopping the curb and crashing into a tree. Smoke billowed out from under the hood as a man opened the door and flung himself onto the ground. She watched, a hand over her mouth and tears in her eyes, as the man drank stagnant water from a puddle left over from last night's rain.

Automobiles continued to crash into each other along the streets. Startlingly, people inside climbed out as if nothing was wrong. Samantha's stomach twisted as she saw a man with a piece of bone sticking out from his left shin. Blood smeared across the sidewalk behind him as he dragged himself to a spilled garbage can. The man then plucked out a rotten apple core and began eating.

"No, no. This can't be happening!" Samantha whispered to herself as she picked up her pace.

Her lab was just at the end of the road. If she could make it there and find out what changed in her viral DNA, she may just be able to stop the virus in its tracks before it took greater hold.

Samantha's heart pounded quickly in her chest as she reached her lab and pulled out her keycard, quickly realizing that security had programmed the lock incorrectly, causing her to remain locked out.

After several swipes, the card still refused to read. Each red light mocked her as she was quickly running out of time.

You caused this. You are why these people are suffering. You do nothing but ruin everything, Samantha thought to herself as she continued to swipe.

"Come on! Come on!" Samantha repeated as she pulled on the glass doors.

Nothing. They refused to budge.

"Ugh, fuck this!"

She scanned around intently and quickly found what she needed, a large rock sitting off to one side of the door, purchased in an attempt to make the landscaping look attractive. Samantha picked up the rock and held a strong grip before swinging it as hard as she could at the doors.

The alarms shrieked as the glass shattered and spilled onto the ground. Samantha moved quickly, ignoring the way the shards bit into the heels of her feet. She needed to get to her notes. She needed to see what went wrong with Lasactka.

She raced down the hallway to her office, flicked on the light, and pushed over her bookshelf, tearing apart binder after binder until she found the one she was looking for. With the binder flipped open and fear instilling in her, Samantha traced the words with her finger.

"Fuck," she whispered, defeated, as her heart stopped.

CHAPTER 3
THE CREATION OF LASACTKA

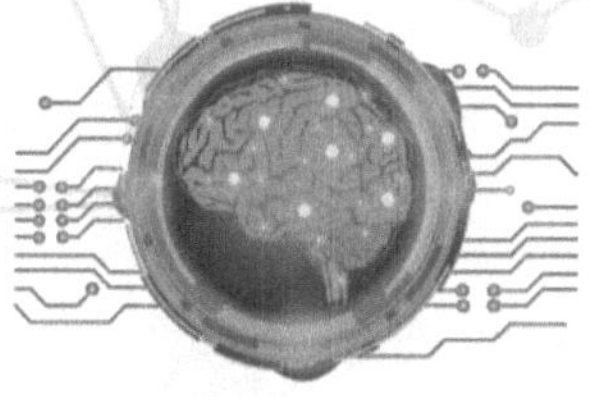

Year 2080

"ALL PASSENGERS, please be seated as we prepare for our arrival at Tenzing Hillary Airport in Lukla, Nepal. As always, remember to brace yourselves and hold on for your lives," the flight attendant announced.

Samantha Mare had taken some time off after graduation to climb to the summit of Mount Everest, her biggest goal since she was a child. She had always watched documentaries and looked up images on the Internet, in awe of the beautiful peak of the tallest mountain in the world.

She spent her past ten years training for this day and had been saving up for over a decade to pay for this experience. She couldn't remember the last time she went on vacation or even out for a drink with her friends.

She was ready. Nothing could stand in her way now as she neared close to her destiny. She could see the beautiful height of the mountain and already pictured herself climbing up.

"All passengers, please do not unbuckle your seatbelts. I repeat, please do not unbuckle your seatbelts. Passengers, please hold on tight and do not panic! I REPEAT, DO NOT PANIC AND DO NOT MOVE!"

Samantha's thoughts dissipated at the sound of a screaming flight attendant as she quickly realized what was happening.

The pilot had landed seconds too late at the world's shortest airport runway, rising at a height of over 9,000 feet in the air, the nose of the aircraft tipping over the edge of a tall cliff toward the ground far below.

Samantha was one of ten others on the small aircraft, all part of the tour she had signed up for to climb the mountain. Her heart was pounding as she looked out the tiny window beside her and saw the world around her rocking back and forth as the plane continued to dangle off the edge of the cliff.

"PASSENGERS! DO NOT PANIC!" the flight attendant screamed again.

But panicked they did, screaming their last words and prayers as they saw their entire lives flash before their eyes.

"Alright, passengers, listen closely. Everyone slowly unbuckle your seatbelts, and on the count of three, run toward the back of the aircraft. We are going to try to tip this plane back onto the runway. Ready, one… two… three… Go!"

With that, all the passengers bolted toward the back of the

plane. However, their haphazard scurry only rocked the jet even more, and it eventually tipped off the edge of the runway and headed straight down.

Samantha closed her eyes as those around her continued to scream and cry. On her way down, she immediately regretted all the decisions she had ever made in her life that led her up to this moment.

"Why did I choose to go on this trek instead of staying home and finding a job?!" she cried to herself.

Samantha had just graduated from Highland University with a PhD in Neuroscience, specializing in human intelligence.

After seven years of diligence, she watched all her classmates go off to interviews and the start of their new careers while she decided to pack her bags and board a plane. However, during this moment, she lamented not having played it safe as she knew her life was coming to an end.

Crash!

"Several days have passed since the crash landing of flight 783 from Kathmandu to Lukla, Nepal. Ten passengers, two pilots, and one flight attendant all boarded the small aircraft early morning last Tuesday, plummeting over 9,000 feet into the ground due to a mishap in the pilot's landing flaw and so far, only a fraction of the bodies have been found. There were no survivors. More to come later tonight."

The sun began to set. The wind picked up against the mountains, and the temperature dropped. A piece of the broken wing from aircraft 783 began to rattle, struggling to budge as the thing below it attempted to push it off.

"Ugh," Samantha groaned as she looked around her environment after pushing the aircraft wing off her.

Her head spun and throbbed, and her chest ached with each new breath.

Maybe I would've been better off dead, she thought as she

blinked rapidly and tried to get a bearing on her surroundings.

A dark blur passed quickly across her vision.

"Hello?" she screamed. "Is anyone there? Is everyone okay!? Is anyone alive?"

She continued to shout until she realized that she was potentially the only survivor left. Cold and lost, she wondered what she should do. She searched around for her bag, but it was nowhere in sight. The crash had caused parts of the destroyed plane to ricochet throughout the valleys and rivers of the mountains.

Hopeless, Samantha walked toward the direction that seemed the safest, toward the peaks. She had no money, no passport, no food, and part of her wished she died in the crash. For days on end, she trudged through the Himalayan mountains, fighting bright sunshine and snowstorms while trying to stay alive.

Since she had decided to embark on this trip during off-season, there was no one in sight for her to call for help. Three weeks passed, and she still found herself alone in the alps, sleeping in caves and keeping warm by building her own fire.

However, one day, everything changed. The cave she presumed was just another hole in the wall turned out to be the entrance leading to an underground tunnel.

"Hello!" Samantha yelled as she walked down a hollow tunnel, her voice echoing behind her. "Is anyone here?"

She walked further down the tunnel and soon came face to face with a wooden door that read, HYGOLTZ: DR. FARROW'S LAB.

Dr. Farrow? Samantha thought. *I know about him. He won the first Synapselligence Award in 2035 for his invention of a microchip that functioned as a brain independent of the body. However, shortly after he received his award, he disappeared from the face of the Earth and was never heard from again. Most suspected that he had somehow transferred his own brain into the chip and committed suicide as a result of it.*

"Who's knocking on my door!?" a faint cry came through from the other side.

"Hello? Dr. Farrow? My name is Samantha Mare. My plane crashed about 80 miles of here, and I'm lost with no food or money. Can I please borrow your phone so I can call for help?" Samantha pleaded.

Samantha walked into the lab after realizing the door was left unlocked and saw numerous yak brains in glass jars. Part startled, part horrified, she was fascinated to learn more.

"What is this?" she asked.

"Dear, I do not have a phone, but my assistant can help you wire wherever and whatever you need in the back," Dr. Farrow answered as if he did not hear her.

"Dr. Farrow, what is all this?" Samantha asked again, curious to learn more about these yak brains.

"These, my child, are yak brains," Dr. Farrow answered.

"What are they for?"

"People, ignorant folk, they all laugh at my work because they don't understand. For years, decades, I have spent my life creating the impossible, changing the world, and people laugh. People are too stupid to understand greatness. People are too dumb to understand life-changing inventions even if they slap them in their stupid faces."

"What are you creating this time? Yak brains. Ambitious."

"The Lasactka virus, guaranteed to make people less stupid, guaranteed to make people understand greatness, guaranteed to make people understand that the world is changing, making people realize that they need to keep up.

The Lasactka virus injects into the brains of individuals and increases their intelligence as quickly as you can blink your eye. People are not stupid because they are genetically stupid; people are stupid because they are genetically lazy. Lasactka gives people the knowledge without the work."

"Wow, that's really incredible. If you can get this virus to attach, it'll change humanity forever. I worked on creating a virus during my grad school years, a virus that could potentially repair dyslexia. Unfortunately, I was never able to figure out the right host to extract it from."

"You, you a scientist?"

"I received my PhD in neuroscience a few months back. Before that, I was working as an assistant scientist in a laboratory that specialized in early-onset dementia."

"You, you be my protégé. It is very difficult working here in the mountains. Nobody comes. Nobody helps me. I'm too old to keep running around. You help me develop virus."

Despite being desperate to go home and forget this nightmare of a trip ever happened, Samantha was also curious to see more of Dr. Farrow's virus. This could hypothetically work. If he could successfully create this strain, society would be unstoppable. All the greatest minds merged into one can create a world capable of endless feats.

"Yes, I will stay," Samantha responded confidently.

CHAPTER 4
THE APOCALYPSE

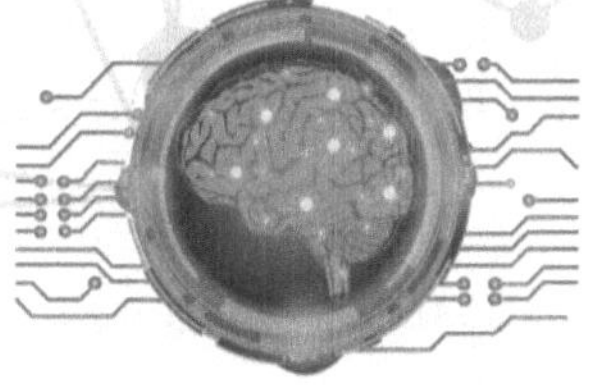

Year 2086

"It has been 75 days since the deadly Himalayan Lasactka was unleashed into the world, creating mayhem, and modern technology and supplies are beginning to dwindle fast. Scientists are forgetting how to create vaccines. Technicians are forgetting how electricity and water systems operate, and leaders of large corporations are quickly being overrun by their chaotic juvenile workers! We are seeing more and more people die by the hour, and there is no one left intelligent enough to stop this pandemic!"

The cold air bites into Miles's skin. It is a lonely and quiet night, but his heart pounds noisily with every swerve he makes. His eyes and ears are on the lookout for "the infected." A stray branch, which hangs from a tree, drops beside his car, and his heart skips a bit in surprise. There is no time to take chances now; the infected may be hiding anywhere.

"It's just a stupid branch," he mutters and drives on.

The apocalypse has been escalating steadily for months now, leading to a full demise of the nation within a matter of weeks. Most people knew the situation was horrific, but many remained in full denial that it would not fall to total destruction of societal structures.

The street in his peripheral vision is completely deserted. He can see smoke arising from the distance. The deafening sound of police and fire truck sirens that had dominated the previous nights have finally abated. The authorities are probably all infected now too, leaving no one left to maintain order.

For him, constantly being on the move means constantly surviving; if he stays in a place for too long, the infected can smell him out and, in a best-case scenario, turn him into an infected. Although his backpack is filled with knives, guns, and other weapons, he knows he is dead meat if he ever gets overpowered by a group of the infected so, the best he can do is to keep avoiding them.

However, this mayhem did not start out like this. He was not always on the run. The world was not always facing an apocalypse, until few weeks ago, when a deadly Himalayan virus was unleashed into human society.

Miles Silver doesn't know the complete backstory to the virus, but he had heard rumors about its creator before he went on the move. Whoever created this invisible force of lethalness had intended for it to spike human intelligence, enhance the greater good of the society, and increase the knowledge of everyone without the effort of having to lift a finger. But it backfired colossally; it went straight for the cerebrum of humans and degenerated them, turning them into zombies and imbeciles.

Reasoning and logic no longer existed as fights broke out throughout the country. There were more accidents as people were no longer aware of the consequences of their actions, and morality had become just another word in the dictionary. Humans now yearned for each other's flesh and blood. Human rot lay wasted on the streets. Those who were not infected by the virus died of hunger as food was no longer being produced or transported.

Within five weeks, country after country went down in disarray as civilians stabbed each other, razed cars and buildings to the ground. There were no leaders left to uphold law and order.

Modern technology had never seen anything like it. Scientists could not bar themselves from the virus long enough to study and create vaccines. They were turned into victims before they even saw it coming, popularly known as "the infected." Plenty of people died by the hour, and there was no one intelligent enough to stop the pandemic.

Except for Miles, but it was too late. The world has passed its redemption stage, and the only thing left for Miles was to run. It took a long time for Miles to get used to the new modus operandi of things; he had hoped that the new order of society was just a temporary fad, and life would soon turn back to normal. Boy, was he wrong.

However, when the virus infected and took over the lives of his parents, his friends, his neighbors (the nice, elderly lady next door and the petulant old man in the complex below him who always pounded at his ceiling whenever he turned the music above silent), and even the charming waitress who always seemed eager and excited to take his order, it was as sure as dawn that the virus had come to stay.

He struggled to pull himself away from his current life, loving every moment of it, from the memories to the experiences to the joys, and he didn't want to leave them all behind.

So, as he perused his luxury condo, adorned with navy blue walls and gold-plated paperweights, he looked at his belongings (which were all of high value and very sentimental to him) for the final time before he embarked on his journey. He knew there was nothing he could do to save the world. Humanity had so much potential. Now it's all going to be over. There was nothing left for him to do but walk away.

Only thing left to save was himself, and that was what he did. Even if he was infected, the symptoms didn't set in, not yet anyway. Before he becomes incapable of thinking clearly, he needed to get to the bomb shelter he found in the isolated nowhere while traveling through the bleak winter of Siberia. That was his only way to survive.

———

He remembers the last conversation he had with a human, a proper one. Miles just resumed work after a sabbatical, unaware and ignorant of the turmoil the virus had caused and was excited to reunite with his colleagues once again.

The sight he was met with was a horrendous one, not the celebratory party he had expected. His boss, who used to be prim and proper, was almost stark naked and feasting on what seemed like the body of one of his colleagues. Everyone had the same characteristics; all mumbling nonsense, all feasting on dead human bodies like they were zombies. It was a scary sight to behold. He tried to talk to one of them, hoping they remembered him enough to spare him his life.

"Run!" he heard one of the people on the office grounds scream.

"Sorry, what? These are my colleagues; I can't leave them like this. I have to talk to them and bring them to their senses," Miles shouted back.

"They're not your colleagues, not anymore. They're different people now; they have been infected by the virus, their brains all changing. They can no longer tell the difference between friend or foe. Once they get to you, you're done for."

Miles took a glance over at the guy speaking to him. He was like them too, but slightly less naked and still somewhat humane. He didn't get it. It didn't make any sense.

"How…how come you're not like them? You're infected, aren't you? Shouldn't you be trying to eat me?"

"The virus has not multiplied in my brain yet, but you better get the fuck out of here before it does!"

At once, Miles felt sorrow for the guy. Here he was trying to help him when he didn't have to. Miles knew he had to extend an offer in return, despite his desire for a solitary life.

"Let me help you. You see, I have a camp in…"

"Don't even bother; the symptoms will soon catch up with me. It is only a matter of time. I can't be saved. Just run! Your life depends on it," the man replied, cutting him short.

And so, Miles did. He ran as if he would never run again. He was terrified to see what the world had become.

However, before he reached his condo, he took a detour at his favorite stall to top up his groceries, preparing for his long expedition to Siberia. What he saw there still shocks him to this day: everything cleared off and burnt down. Only rubbles were left of the spoil. He didn't even see the owner, Mr. Munch, who was usually always there. Bright and early to greet his customers.

It felt like one of those heists he watched when he was a young teenager. It was so unreal that the same thing was now happening in real life. The streets were also decorated with roasted car shells and blown-up corpses, as entrails hung from streetlights like festive streamers. Truly, the world had gone mad.

———

A sight cuts into his train of thought. Peering out a few meters away, his greatest fear comes charging at him: the infected. They stagger toward him in zombie-fashion, hunger written over their faces. There appearances are too unsettling to even begin to describe. Their faces wretched, enough to make Miles vomit.

Over on his left, he sees some of the infected roaming, inspecting each sign, car, and piece of trash they pass as if they had never seen such strange objects. One of them begins picking away at his fingers, peeling off skin until blood drips rapidly onto the ground.

A few others appear lost as they awkwardly run into each other, yelling out nonsensical opinions. That is what the virus does.

Although the horde consists of children and adults alike, they are not human, not anymore. Dribble and pus fall from various sides of their bodies as they trudge forward. Miles is caught in a conundrum.

To go back is to return to where he came from, which was dangerous enough, and to go forward, where the infected is coming from, is to risk getting bitten or killed. But one thing is sure: this horde is all that's left around here. He could crush them with his tires, or he could…

SNAP!

One of the infected bangs heavily at his window. There is no time to think; he has to take action, now! He reverses with a force that leaves one of the infected flailing on the ground.

He surprises them and can't wait to release more from his bag of adrenaline.

He abruptly swerves left, and one of the infected who has been trailing him smashes against the rear of his Sedan. Another comes at him bearing weapons; for that, he turns his car in the direction of the monster, colliding with him destructively. A blunt thud can be heard as the "thing" hits the passenger door of Miles's car and drops to the ground. Miles wipes his sweat off his brows, and a dark spot forms under his arms.

When will this madness end? He turns on his wipers; blood streaks across the windshield like drops of rain.

Another one of the infected almost catches him off-guard, a maniac on a motorcycle following him with a rifle. He would have nailed him too if Miles hadn't noticed the lone figure through his rearview mirror. Hoping to startle him, he slams on his brakes, and the maniac smashes against the car, the rifle flying out of his hands.

Miles then abruptly turns left, and suddenly, everything becomes quiet again while he cruises down a deserted alleyway.

This is so strange, Miles thinks to himself.

Just a few weeks ago, the infected were high and mighty; they were respected people in the society. Now, they are part of a plague, primitively murdering each other with rocks, and eating their peers and neighbors like zombies.

Even though the world is dealing with a nuclear doom, it doesn't mean the layers of humankind have peeled off. It doesn't mean the ability to think and reason have already faded. How could humankind have eroded so quickly? Had the layer of civilization really been that thin?

Society had clearly broken down even before anything really happened. Was intelligence just a mask for people's guilty pleasures, using this outbreak as an excuse to enact on them?

All is clear now, or so he hopes. He had killed all the infected he encountered.

As he cruises onto a clear road with a small backpack filled with little food supply, he prays to the gods that he doesn't encounter any of the infected before arriving at his camp.

CHAPTER 5
ESCAPE TOWARD TRAGEDY

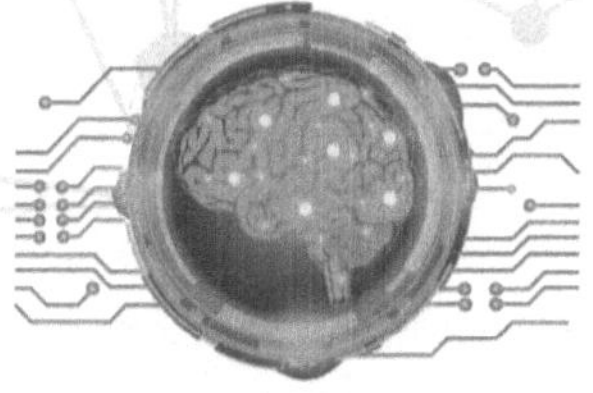

FINALLY REACHING the end of the road, fifty short miles from where he needs to be, Miles pulls over his car and begins to walk toward his camp, hoping he won't be murdered or eaten along the way. Everything around him is other-worldly quiet, not like he had expected anyone to be around.

They are all either already gone or had become too swine-like to even think of escaping the chaos.

He has gotten to the end of the road; the rest needs to be reached by foot. He steps out of his car, locks it, and put the keys in his back pocket. He quietly moves, careful to not attract attention. He anxiously looks around for more of the infected, but none are to be seen.

Although he does not expect anyone to be around, the quiet is unbearable for him. At that moment, his phone decides to ring. He wasn't expecting anyone to be alive, much less call him on a day like this. He steels himself as he slowly checks his phone and wonders what bad news it will bring this time.

Alas, it is only his alarm. He forgot to switch it off since the last time he went into the office. He turns it off promptly and continues moving. With only a measly 10% left, he needs to preserve his battery in case of an emergency. He chuckles to himself. That idea sounded as dumb as hoping anyone is still alive. He keeps going, until he reaches his safe destination where he is sure to die alone in peace.

The wind is now freezing as Miles continues to walk, his teeth chattering in his skull.

Is this what it sounds like when the infected masticates on skeletons? Miles wonders as he sees a moving shadow on his right.

Startled, he glances up and sees a human corpse dangling upside down from a large oak tree, staring at him with eyes wide open and blood trickling from his mouth to his forehead, a grim smile forever frozen in death. Cold fear runs down Miles's spine. Shit.

There are thousands of other human corpses lined up in the same fashion: all hanging upside down and donning darkness, their hands crossed over their chests. The apocalypse has eradicated more people than he will ever know.

This begs the question about the foolproofness of society. Is society as solid as the Founding Fathers claimed? Can an external factor just dismantle the balance of the modern world and make it come crushing down like a deck of cards?

Despite the alarming sight, Miles keeps on walking. His heart races with fear, and his palms are coated with sweat.

However, he consoles himself with the fact that they are all dead and can do him no harm.

But that comfort suddenly vanishes as one of the dangling corpses opens her eyes. She unfolds her arms and begins to flail them at Miles as he walks under the row of dead. He spots a backpack beneath the tree and hopes it contains supplies he can use.

The tangled arms of the woman try to grab hold of Miles's locks as he leans over to snatch the bag, startling him and scaring him in the process. She also tries to grab part of his body, her decomposing hands grazing his left cheek instead. Miles cocks his gun and slowly lifts his head. As he aims to shoot, he freezes in his tracks as a familiar face greets him with a bloody smile.

"Wait, Sarah?" he asks the infected body, fully aware that she will not be able to reply.

"Die, incompetent human, Die!" Sarah, or the thing that resembled Sarah, growls as she tries to grab a patch of his hair.

Luckily, Miles is able to dodge her but still cannot stop staring. That "infected" over there is not Sarah; it is definitely some sort of monster that had consumed her.

There is a slight madness in her eyes that is close to hysteria. Her body is covered in bruises and wounds, blood dripping from her gouged eyes. A part of her left ear is missing, and her body looks close to crumbling. However, this lunacy is not unusual. Right before his most recent partner turned, she had also exuded hysteria.

He does not hesitate to shoot; he brings the gun to her face, and it explodes with a single click. Sarah crumbles into debris.

Several memories of Sarah flash through his mind. For a long time, while he was still a fitness freak, he used to pass by her every morning during his daily jogs, the once-beautiful park, adorned with a large pond, adorable ducks, and pretty roses, has now turned into a murky swamp: an aftermath of the apocalypse.

"Nice day, isn't it?" she would always say as Miles responded with affirmation.

They used to jog together, spanning a large breadth. Sometimes, they would take deep breaks and gulp down water from their bottles, finishing it and gasping for breath because of the speed at which they swallowed.

Other times, they went on short walks, conversing in between. Because of walks like these, Miles discovered that Sarah's last name was Letman, and at the age of 35, she was only able to conceive once before having a miscarriage.

She also had a husband, but they divorced after two years. She was a teacher at Brightside Elementary, and despite all the misfortunes she had endured in life, she always managed to greet others with a smile. Miles always listened intently, finding her experiences and stories fascinating. After several months, their relationship began to blossom, starting with a kiss that soon became more intimate, the affair that Miles always wanted.

Sarah, or whoever she is, is no longer the person who used to greet him with stimulating stories every morning. This is no longer the person who drove him to the emergency room when he scraped his knee during a cold winter run.

You see, the infected are still human. Roughly four months ago, a deadly virus was intentionally released from the Himalayan mountains known as "Lasactka."

This virus was intended to enhance the greater good of society, increasing the knowledge of everyone without the added effort. The creator of the virus, Mare, as they called her, had expected Lasactka to construct the greatest society known to man, accomplishing endless achievements and generating knowledge far beyond anyone could ever know.

However, unbeknownst to everyone, this virus eventually went awry, and shortly after it was released into the world, it dissolved into the cerebrums of the population and caused everyone to develop mental retardation.

Fights and accidents broke out as people were no longer aware of consequences and morality. Reasoning and logic no longer existed as riots broke out all over the country.

Within five short weeks, country after country combusted, civilians stabbing each other and lighting cars and buildings on fire. There were no leaders left to promote social order.

The people had forgotten how to manufacture food and generate power, leaving cities to rot in starvation and desolation. The entire world was either freezing over or burning down, and Miles was stuck in the middle of the two.

Silver was one of the last humans to become infected, or so he claimed. However, since symptoms set almost immediately, he knew he didn't have much time before he became completely incapable of even thinking clearly.

The only way for him to survive is if he makes his way to the bomb shelter in the isolated nowhere he had discovered months ago while traveling through the bleak winter of Siberia.

Scanning the remaining barren trees, Miles sees more of the diseased beginning to awake. Nervous that one of them might flail at him again, Miles quickly snatches up the backpack as if his life depended on it, shooting anyone and anything that moves.

What are these things? Are they really evil, or are they simply ignorant to social order? Do they no longer remember who they were or who they recognized after they are infected? Sarah sure didn't seem to notice him, or did she notice but attempted to kill him anyway?

Too many questions rush through his mind. He must remain concentrated on one goal and one goal only: to get out of here before anyone else tries to kill him.

CHAPTER 6
ISOLATED AND ALONE

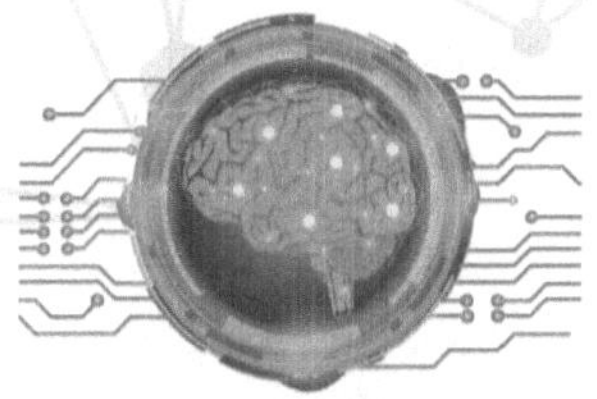

AFTER MANY BLEAK days of trudging through snow and shooting anyone who stood in his path, Miles finally reaches his shelter, which remains untouched, just as he had left it.

There is no one else around, not like he expected there to be; the apocalypse has done its job of eliminating over half the planet.

At first glance, the camp seems empty, the shelter he preserved for himself. But on closer look, through the opening, there appears to be someone inside, in HIS camp. Fear grips Miles by the shirt; he has only been gone for a few weeks, and there is already a stranger in his shelter. The worst part, he isn't sure if the person inside is a living dead.

Summoning his courage, he gingerly walks into the camp, sighing in relief when he sees the man lying frozen still. He isn't sure how long the man has been dead for, but given the mottling of his skin, he had to have died over two weeks ago.

For several hours, Miles battles with what to do: he can either drag him out, or he can abandon camp and keep walking so the others don't come sniffing around. With his luck though, he'd probably end up freezing in the snow before seeing any shelter in sight.

Dragging the man out to fend for himself may seem like the obvious answer, but what if the body's still contaminated? What if he had been symptomatic right before he died, and the virus still lingers inside him? Touching the corpse would mean walking to his own death.

Weighing his options, he digs out some spare gloves from his backpack and slowly drags the dead man from his shelter, burning both his gloves and the body before heading back inside.

He pitches down his heavy bag, filled with a couple cans of cold beans, and kicks off his shoes. His feet had become irritated with callouses and blisters from the long distance.

He gathers some wood to create a blaze, melting snow over the flames to create water for a shower. He then devours three cans of cold beans and passes out in front of the open kindle.

As he tries to relax on his thin sheet, his leg hits something hard. At first thought, it seemed like an ordinary stone, but as he digs deeper, he pulls out a journal dating back over 200 years.

After reading several pages, Miles discovers that over two centuries ago, the world had been plagued with a similar virus, turning into an apocalypse and destroying all of humanity. Whoever wrote this journal must have traveled far and away to escape like Miles had.

Shock washes over Miles as he swipes through several pages with amazement. The owner of this journal was clearly an artist, the book filled with caricatures of zombies, people eating each other, no food, riots, and fights. There were also caricatures of the owner himself, explaining how he went from being a stout, short man to malnourished within months. Down to the cause, the effect and impact, they were all the same.

Miles doesn't need a brain to guess that the man had starved to death, like he soon will. History always repeats itself because society never learns. There is nothing to do with the book now anyways; the earth cannot be redeemed, and he is only waiting to die, peacefully.

Waking up in the middle of the night to a burnt-out flame and reoccurring nightmares of the infection, Miles lies on top of his blanket, trying to come to terms with reality. Every morning in this isolated shelter is starting to become the same: horrifying dreams with an even worse reality.

Every morning, he continues to force himself to get up even though there is no longer any reason to do so. What's the point? He has no motivation to do anything anymore, living included. There are no longer plans or goals to be sought after except to simply survive.

He once lived a daily routine, where he woke up around noon every morning, worked out, and ate a hearty breakfast before going off to work. Now, he sits in this dungeon and waits for either his death or his impending tragic transformation, unsure of which would be the worst way to go.

His days now consist of waking up, building a fire, and eating some beans before falling back asleep next to the flames. The wind becomes more brutal with each passing day, the clouds creating an overcast in the dark grey sky, serving as a constant reminder that catastrophe has befallen upon humanity.

Miles had wasted his entire life saving up for a luxurious home, only to end up living in one made of stone.

Unfortunately, money no longer means anything when there is nothing left for it to be spent on. He couldn't even bear to splurge on new boots that were free of holes because he wanted a mantle made of marble. As his toes begin to freeze in the frigid snow, he realizes how poor his choices had been.

I should have lived when I had the chance. Everyone told me to stop waiting until I'm old to begin living. Heck, now I won't even have the chance to become old.

Loneliness begins to set in during his endless days in the shelter. Miles craves for companionship, but there is no one left alive to grant him his wish. Apart from food, human touch is all he wants. If he doesn't go crazy from the spread of the virus, he may as well go crazy from the sequestration and isolation.

However, he has his doubts: what if someone comes to join him and ends up pilfering his food, leaving him high and dry, like those bumbling idiots out there? He had experience with people like that, and he refuses to let that happen again, especially in a pandemic where basic amenities are scarce. He is no fool. It only makes sense that his best chance of surviving, for at least a few more months, is to remain alone.

When he was still in the area chockfull of the infected, although it was unsafe, he got his well-needed companionship. People surrounded him, and he had no cause to complain. He wonders if the virus still lingers, ravaging its terror. He wonders if it's safe to go back home. Maybe he has become the sole survivor on Earth after all, and the virus had turned everyone into cannibals due to lack of food supplies. That certainly seems like a risk he does not want to take, the risk he refuses to take until it is necessary to do so.

On the flip side, he needs food. Miles has enough water, shelter, and firewood to survive the next few months, but his dwindling food supply remains a setback. He wishes he had stocked up on more before his journey, but his options were limited.

Even if this virus has a potential end, he might not make it until then to bask in its celebration. He will soon be known as the idiot who died in a Russian bomb shelter because he was too impatient to wait it out.

All he has achieved with this escape is a postponement of his death for a few more months and sheltered quarantine from all communication, leaving him in complete seclusion. At the start of all this, he had considered himself the lucky one, the one able to escape the chaos, but doubts are now beginning to creep in.

These lingering thoughts continue to wander through his mind as he scuffles his cold feet through the white and fluffy snow. He used to love coming here. Siberia is one of the most wonderful places in the world to escape from the woes of society. Now, it has become a death sentence.

As usual, he tries to determine where the grey sky ends and the equally grey snow begins. And per usual, he is not successful. The ubiquitous never-ending hue of greyness that surrounds him had set in a few weeks after the downfall of humanity, with the hefty temperature drop soon following.

This must be what a nuclear winter feels like. Miles had always heard rumors about it; never did he think he would experience it first-hand.

Angst soon creeps in while nerves rampage through his mind over the shortage of food. It is time to decide, risk contact with the infected humans or remain safe until the food supply is completely drained to the point where he cannot hold out another day.

His main trepidation, however, is that he cannot assume that first contact with the infected world would be successful and lead to replenished food stocks. In fact, it seems rather unlikely.

Nevertheless, common sense refuses to allow him to wait until he is almost starved before initiating a risk; that wouldn't leave enough time to find alternatives. Besides, the thought of seeing people again, despite them being diseased, feels almost too tempting.

With this, he gathers his almost empty bag, with enough room to store a new supply of food if he is lucky, puts out the flame, bundles up in his 12-year-old parka, and makes his way toward civilization.

CHAPTER 7
THE UNEXPECTED ENCOUNTER

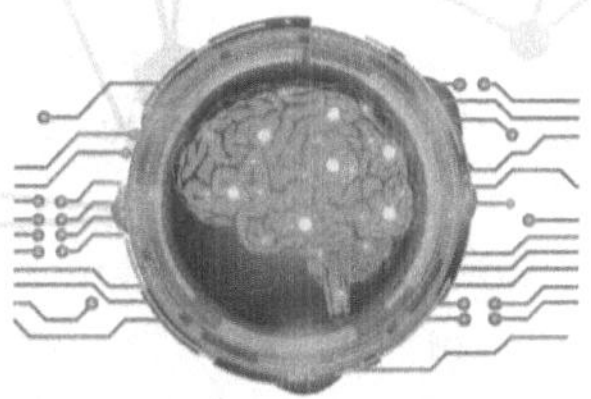

It has been days on this long journey, and over forty dreadful miles later, Miles begins to encounter more than just mountains of snow and ice. Never in his life have barren trees and suspended bodies looked so attractive. Still, most of his surroundings continue to remain disgustingly grey.

The occluded mist clouds his perception, and the brisk strikes of wind brush through the strands of his hair. No way the world could possibly continue to remain this bleak; the nuclear winter would surely crush every last bit of hope humanity had remaining.

A few short ways later, Miles realizes he should have turned back when he had the chance. The existing world is no longer safe, and he stands a higher chance of survival back home in the solitude of his burrow.

However, the thought of encountering people and potential resources is just too enticing.

Maybe I'll run into a potential non-infected. Maybe I can learn more about whether the virus is dying, and maybe I can go back home. I need information. I need some sort of hope.

The closer Miles approaches civilization, the closer he holds his gun to his side as danger is just around the corner. The sky is becoming more and more opaque as he presses on, with haze filling the air, almost to the point where Miles is no longer able to see the decomposing bodies lying behind him.

Further down the road, he approaches a thick barren tree with maybe one or two crusted dead leaves still attached to it, this time, free of corpses. Crouching behind it, he scours for more of the budding diseased and a feasible town to invade before proceeding forward.

Nothing. Nothing, except for darkness. Nothing, except for an absence of all light and all civilization. Shit.

Fearful and still cautious of the evil lurking behind the fog, Miles continues walking until he reaches one of the towns. He approaches a hoard of vultures who had torn into his car, the same location he had left it, leaving him to fend for himself. So much for his plan.

Walking into the once-urban society feels like walking into a post-apocalyptic ghost town. People are colliding into each other as if they are toddlers, cackling and laughing when they tumble in supposed pain.

Miles feels like he had just walked into a preschool of full-grown adults who are forgetting how to accomplish the simplest of tasks. From what he can see, the virus is still causing mayhem. Worse, there is still no food. All the shops have been shut down; shops that were open were still open with reason, there was nothing left.

His stomach begins to rumble louder, and his pounding headache returns, reminding him of his imminent death if he doesn't find some food soon. Whatever glucose is still left in him is deteriorating by the second. The fear of dying evokes fear in Miles, causing him to move further into the city, hoping that, by a stroke of luck, he finds a pack of edibles.

Armed, he saunters deeper into the town, ransacking all the shops he sees. Nothing. Everything had either been stolen or eaten. He considers eating the mottled and rotten carcasses on the ground, but concludes that death by starvation beats death by infection any day. He bows his head in growing disappointment. If only he had paid more attention in the Scouts, he wouldn't need to rely on man-made products to survive.

Night draws near, and the hungry Miles starts to count the seconds to his demise. The owls hoot, as if in preparation for his death. He sits on the curb and reminisces on all the memories when he had thrown away food because of a single strand of hair. There is nothing much to do at this point. Wait for death and hope it comes with ease. When he becomes tired of reminiscing, he switches to tears. Draining his energy on tears means that when death does arrive, he won't be able to fight it.

He can only rest in the solace that he has made it this far, a soldier resting in peace. He had fought a good fight, and dying from starvation would only be another sign of the fallen and corrupt world. The signs of death are already upon him. He can feel his organs eating themselves.

"The time has arrived," he whispers to himself as he falls asleep.

———

The next morning, Miles is surprised to find himself still alive. A little further down the road, he finds a convenience store, demolished and destroyed, with infant-like adults eating tubes of paint and plaster. He walks up and down the aisles just to find all the food packages ripped into and consumed, all but one box of dried pasta. It's his. He needs it. He needs that box of pasta. Miles hadn't eaten carbs in months, and he begins salivating for even one piece.

However, as he begins inching toward it, a grown man rolls over on a beat-up skateboard and begins crunching on his box of pasta like they are potato chips.

Fuck. So much for stocking up, Miles deliberates, infuriated.

Walking a few more blocks down, Miles soon discovers the hell he had expected; the streets are all empty, all desolate, all abolished, with the next closest town 100 miles away.

Just about ready to surrender in despair on his search, he hears a faint cry from a distance: the sound of a woman's voice. She can't be that far away, but should he really risk it?

He already has a short supply of food as is, and he's struggling to desperately scavenge to find anything, even expired food, to keep him alive for a few more months.

Can he really risk bringing in another mouth to feed and shortening his own lifespan that much more?

Miles hears the faint cry sound again, sharper and slower than before.

"Can I really live with myself if I don't act like a decent human being here and save her? What a nightmare! If I save her, I die. If I leave, my conscience kills me anyway. Fuck it," Miles says to himself in defeat as he begins heading toward her direction, continuing to tread until the cry becomes louder and louder.

He eventually reaches the exact location where the voice was heard but sees no one in sight. Miles had expected hordes of the infected to surround some innocent woman, petting her like a porcelain doll, but to his surprise, he finds no one.

"Hello!?" he screams. "Is anyone out here?"

No reply.

"Hello!?" Miles screams again. "Is anyone out here?"

"I can't. I can't. I can't live like this anymore."

Miles hears a docile, but raspy, voice repeat from above his head. He looks up and sees a frail and brittle young woman standing on the ledge of a tall building.

"Hey!" Miles screams. "What are you doing?"

"It's all my fault. It's all my fault. I need to die. I deserve to die!" the voice continues to bellow down toward Miles's direction.

"Hey! It's not your fault. Please step down from the ledge. Let's talk! Come on down!"

"No! Everyone's dying, and it's all my fault."

The woman is clearly hysteric. There is no point in trying to talk any sense into her. She definitely isn't going to come down on her own. Still, Miles has to get her down one way or another. Too many people are dying, and he refuses to let another one die under his watch.

Waiting for just the right moment as she paces left and right on the ledge, Miles fears for the woman's life, as one misstep will cause her to come plummeting down. He slowly raises his gun, making sure to aim at just the right spot, pulls the trigger, and successfully makes the shot, shooting a tranquilizer straight into her neck.

To his demise, the woman does not fall onto the roof of the building as he had expected, instead, she quickly comes plunging down. Fuck.

Luckily, Miles is quick on his feet and catches her limp body right before she smashes into confetti on the concrete sidewalk. Part of him is delighted that she looks like she clearly had been starving. Insensitive, but there is no one left to judge him.

Without thinking, Miles finds great difficulty in trying to carry her back to his shelter, trudging through the thick snow, melted ice quickly seeping into his frayed shoes along the way. About halfway, he wonders how much easier it would be if he had just left her there to die.

For Miles, it is surprising to see another human who hasn't been infected. Does she have a food reserve somewhere? What about the infected? How had she been able to fend them off? She didn't seem like someone who would engage in fisticuffs, so the only other option would've been luck.

For having lived this long, he gave her huge accolades. This also brought about the question of how he would cope from now on. Trusting his own senses almost failed him this time. He had gone in search of food and almost died. He just needs to go back to his camp and eat all he has left while waiting for death to come once and for all. Even if this stranger does have a food reserve, he won't bother her. He won't try to cheat her of what's hers.

Suddenly, he hears a sound. He can sense that something inhumane and strange is coming their way. From the noise, they are not far. The sound grows louder and more intense.

Although the sky is pitch dark, Miles soon hears a hysterical scream that stops just as quickly as it started. Vulgar rampages of cheering soon follow. It dawns on him that there is nothing to be gained here. This place, this society he once called "home," is now a dangerous pit, and the only way out is to run.

CHAPTER 8
THE UNFORESEEN CONNECTION

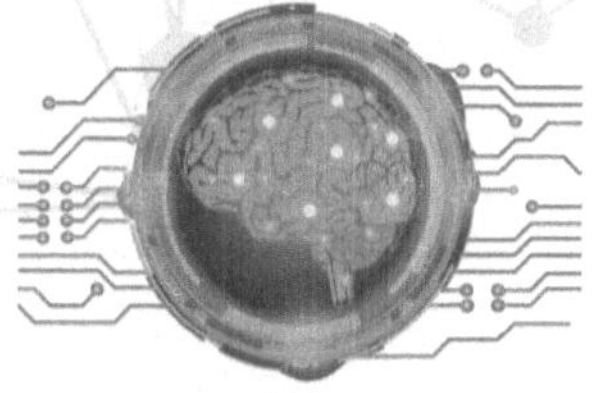

SLAPPING through the bushes and breathing wildly, Miles continues running until he is out of breath. It is a hustle for survival. Run or die. Finally arriving back at his camp, with exploded blisters and scratches covering the soles of his feet, Miles places the frail woman on the asphalt ground of his shelter.

Distracted by his seemingly heroic act in saving her back in town, Miles just notices that the woman is adorned in a bedraggled collection of soaked rags. Everything is tattered, filthy, and difficult for Miles to tell what kind of garment her clothing had once been.

Miles is never good at socializing with others. He grew up without a family; his parents ran out on him when he was just a child and left him with nothing, not even memories. Because of this, he developed a lack of trust toward everyone around him, avoiding people for most of his life.

Whenever someone stood close to him, he developed a strong urge to quickly flee. But, it's not like Miles cannot function at all around other individuals. He is still able to behave relatively normally in the presence of fellow human beings; he just doesn't prefer it.

Interacting with women is even tougher for him. He knows, of course, that it is expected in order to form any kind of relationship with females. He likes sex, quite a lot at that, but he just doesn't like the rest, including the expectations, the commitments, the endless planning of a future, and constantly living a life where he needs to prove himself.

Sadly, those are all aspects of a relationship that most women find crucial and necessary. Fuck women.

As a result, Miles was able to effortlessly and bitterly disappoint every single woman he ever had a relationship with, even though he had never made any promises. On the contrary, as soon as Miles had learned the rules of the game, he warned every single one of them that he would never give into their demands.

Still, many continued to overlook his warnings, convinced they could convert him, but eventually gave up and left, calling Miles an asshole and a bigot.

Now, here he is, the guy unable to live with a woman, suddenly sharing the confined space of a bomb shelter in the middle of nowhere with one. Miles sighs and gently places her unconscious and trembling form onto a thin blanket.

Her body is skeleton-thin, and she has small injuries and large bruises almost everywhere on the face of her skin.

Fortunately, she doesn't look like she is capable of any immediate danger to him, not yet anyway; in fact, Miles doubts she would even survive the night.

As he begins to walk away, he hears a faint sigh from behind him. Surprised, the woman flutters open her eyes briefly and smiles gently at him, whispering "thank you" before drifting back into sleep.

While she slumbers, Miles sits on the ground beside her, watching her sleep while thinking of revised ways to survive his new unforeseen situation, when she suddenly screams and jerks upward with forceful energy as if just awakening from a nightmare. She looks around with wide eyes, confused and disoriented.

Without speaking a single word, she focuses her gaze at Miles, frightened. She doesn't even know this guy's name, and suddenly, she's sitting in a room with him. Her face is jaunt, and from what he could see of her body, she looks near death due to increased starvation, almost like a zombie or some sort. He could barely handle sane women; this one petrifies him.

In attempts to soothe and comfort her, Miles places his hand on top of hers, surprising himself. He usually isn't into human contact, but it seems inhumane of him to not do so.

He watches her eyes wander around the room, stopping when they landed on him. She searches in his eyes, refusing to break contact and mesmerized with his features, leaving Miles feeling scrutinized and uncomfortable.

Rather than pulling out a sharp knife and stabbing him in the chest like Miles had feared, she simply smiles at him once again, weakly, before leaning back down onto her sheet and closing her eyes, tension eliminating from Miles's body.

———

The next morning, Miles finds himself kicking and cursing at what he had done as he leaves the shelter to confirm the safety of his location. How could he have been so foolish, saving a random girl during these hard times, a stranger nonetheless? On the other hand, he continues to excuse himself in how his guilt would've eradicated him otherwise if he had not saved her.

After spending the morning gathering firewood, Miles returns to the shelter to find the woman sitting upright on her blanket, awake and staring straight toward him. To say that situation is awkward would be a gross understatement.

The silence between them becomes brutal, with neither of them speaking a word for a painful stretch of time. He is afraid of saying anything that would trigger the possible murderer inside her while she is frightened he would try to tranquilize her again. Miles continues to stare, standing by the entrance for an awkwardly amount of time like an idiot and pretending not to know what to say when in truth, all he wants is for her to voluntarily leave.

I saved her life. What the hell am I supposed to do now? I can't make any fucking promises about the future. Hell, I don't even know if there is a future, Miles reflects in his mind while grinning at her like a sucker.

To break the silence, he hands her some bacteria-filled water he had dug up from the murky frozen ground, and she starts to drink, shockingly slowly, as Miles had expected her to wolf it down like an animal.

He could not help but continue to gawk at the woman as she downs her drink, suddenly finding her extremely attractive. Once he looked past her bruises and malnutrition, she became a sight to behold.

The long locks he had grabbed hold of to rescue her hung, scraggly and unkempt, down her bare back, revealing more cuts on her cheeks and forehead as she brushes her hair back.

She catches Miles gazing intently at her as she runs her

fingers through her tangled hair, and their eyes lock, breaking when she giggles and turns her head away seconds later, leaving Miles feeling even more awkward.

I'm fine. I'm fine, right? I sure don't need a companion. My situation is stable for the next several months or so to come, or at least it was. I already saved her life. I owe her nothing. I did my duty.

My only goal now is to get rid of her as soon as possible. Hell, I would even be a gentleman and drop her off wherever she wants as soon as she is strong enough, Spain, Africa, Peru, it doesn't matter, as long as she doesn't stay here.

Everyone still alive at this point has their own problems. Surely, she would understand if I don't want to burden myself with hers. I had already done an irrationally valiant act by risking my life to rescue hers.

Yes, dropping her on some road with those "things" doesn't sound completely justifiable. I guess I could part with a few weeks of supplies so she could defend herself on the road, but no way would I halve my entire life expectancy by sharing more than that. No way, that is too much.

Shit, is she still watching me? Exactly how long have I been in thought? Time no longer means anything to me anymore. Life is just stagnant now, with each day exactly like the previous one.'

"Come to a conclusion?" the woman asks with a hoarse voice, breaking Miles's stream of thought.

Her fragile condition had made her voice sound scratchy and thin, but Miles is still amazed by her calmness. After all, this is life or death for her.

"Um...," he begins to speak. *How the hell do I tell someone whom I had rescued that I'm thinking of ditching her the first chance I get?*

"It's okay," she responds softly, almost as if she could read every thought inside his mind.

"What?" he responds ignorantly, pretending to feign innocence to his fatal thoughts

"Do whatever you need to do. It's okay. I'd be dead by now anyway without your help. To me, you can do no wrong despite what you decide. I'll always be grateful for you. You'll always be my hero."

Miles strains to understand her as her weak tone makes it a bit difficult to hear, but what he could hear, made him feel like shit. Her hero? That shouldn't change a thing though. He still needs to do what needs to be done. He stands up and turns around, ready to say something, anything to light up the dreadful situation.

However, upon opening his mouth, only silence is heard, mostly because he could not think of anything to say. Not like it matters anyway as her eyes had quickly closed, and she had fallen fast asleep, probably faking it to make things easier for him. Damn.

Hero. You'll always be my hero. She had said in that thin, hollow voice of hers.

Shit, he ruminates. *Heroes are resilient and strong, and they do heroic deeds for other people without a single selfish thought toward themselves. That's exactly what had not happened. Never did, never would.*

The more he thinks about it, the more Miles wonders if he had ever done anything for anyone but himself. Sure, he had cleaned the dishes when it was his turn on those rare occasions when he was in a relationship. If he truly is a hero, he would have saved Ms. Bauer from next door, an innocent old lady and probably the closest Miles had to a friend, but instead, he left her back home to live out her destined fate with the rest of the infected.

Pssh, hero, more like the opposite is what it is, he continues to ponder. *So why did I rescue this woman over all the rest, depriving those poor weirdly-dressed islanders of their, well, whatever they could have used her for, rather than using her as a distraction for*

my escape? And incidentally, draining me of my least-replaceable commodity, food, thus shortening my life?

Why did I feel like I wouldn't be able to live with myself if I had left her there? I left Ms. Bauer, and I don't feel the slightest of guilt about that. Perhaps my fatal loneliness really did overtake my logic, and I saved her out of pure selfishness for companionship.

After his long internal dialogue, Miles concludes his "heroic act" was simply a rational, self-serving motive, not in the least chivalrous. He could live with that. Having settled his internal conundrum, he curls up in his corner of the room.

Just before falling asleep, a stray thought swiftly crosses his mind, *It really is rather nice to know that there's someone in the world who doesn't think you're an asshole, someone who might, someday, perhaps even admire you.*

CHAPTER 9
INTERACTIONS WITH THE STRANGER

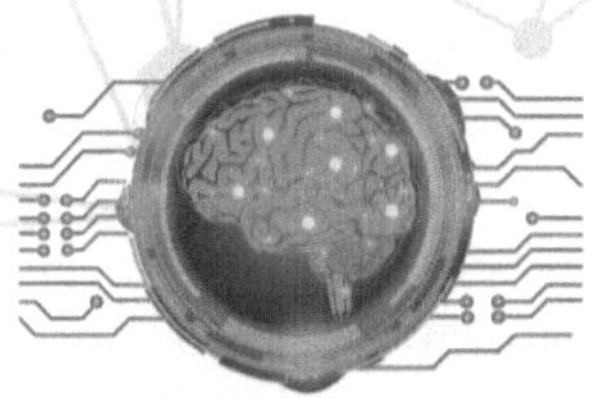

THE NEXT MORNING sees Miles rising bright and early. That sounds normal enough, right? It's not. Waking up early has always been his Achilles Heel, and he would become infuriated and violent at anyone who tried to force him to do so.

With one eye still sealed shut, he stumbles over to his stash of supplies and opens a can of cold beans with his pocketknife. However, before Miles could dig in, he finds that he is being watched.

Damn, he thinks to himself. *I thought I was the only one awake.*

Not wanting to seem rude, even though he continues to stand there cumbersomely, about to pour some beans into his mouth, he turns toward her and begrudgingly asks if she would like any, secretly hoping she declines.

"I'll eat anything I can get my hands on. That's what you do when you've almost starved to death," she replies with hungry eyes.

"Oh, I see."

"You better hide what you have though. It will take all my willpower not to gulp everything you own down at once." She lightly jokes and chuckles, hoping to break the tension.

"I see. Just tell me how much you want, okay? No point in wasting supplies if we don't need to," Miles speaks with obvious resentment and mild displeasure toward this living being who needs his food for survival.

"Okay." She smiles after realizing the man in front of her isn't relishing in her humor. "You're really sweet, you know that?"

"I'm Miles, by the way."

Miles's paranoia begins to make him think her benevolent words are simply ploys to get him to let his guard down.

No way could he or would he ever let the words of someone, especially a woman, overtake his trusted instincts. He has survived long enough on his own; now is not the time to let go of what he knows.

"Sam."

"Nice to meet you. How are you?" Miles forcefully responds, fully knowing he sounds like an idiot by asking how she is under such harsh circumstances, but what else is he supposed to say during introductions?

He couldn't say "glad you're not dead, now get out" because that would be "uncivilized."

"So, why'd you try to kill yourself?" he asks to cover his word fart, catching himself too late for his insensitive question.

"It's my fault that everyone… you know what, just forget it. I don't really want to talk about that right now," Sam responds with an anemic smile.

Suddenly at a loss for words, she begins to cry, with no tears coming out. Miles can't seem to even begin imagining what had happened to her to cause her to almost commit suicide. Again, his thoughts are met with silence.

Sam quickly pulls herself together and looks him in the eyes again.

Here it comes, Miles dreadfully voices in his head. *She's going to say something that will make it impossible to get rid of her. I need her to go!'*

"Thank you, Miles," she articulates.

"For what?"

"For saving me. I know that was a threatening decision for you."

She's right, and they both know it, so Miles remains inaudible. The bonding he had feared has already started. This being is no longer 110lbs of needy humanity; this human being is Sam, a living soul with a life and a name.

Still, Miles is determined not to deter from doing what needs to be done. His life depends on his self-discipline.

"Don't worry, Miles. Whatever you plan to do with me, it's still better than the fate you've rescued me from."

Damn, is she reading my mind or something? Does she know I'm trying to throw her as bait to those creatures out there?

Not knowing what to say that wouldn't potentially offend her again, Miles remains inelegantly still until he unexpectedly dozes off.

Several hours later, Miles wakes up, startled when he realizes Sam had been roaming around unsupervised while he snoozed. Clearly, he is still very alive, so maybe she isn't out to eradicate him after all.

He looks down at his torso and touches a soft blanket covering him that had not been there before he fell asleep.

"Sam," Miles whispers as he looks around the shelter and sees her nowhere in sight. "Maybe she left. Maybe she decided she was a burden and chose to take herself out of my equation."

Trying to hold back his presumed excitement, he pulls his parka over his shoulders and exits the shelter. To his unfortunate surprise, he sees Sam warming her cold hands over an open fire. She sees him and could almost predict the thoughts running through his mind as sweat travels down Miles's temple, despite the frozen tundra they are immersed in.

"You can trust me," Sam reassures Miles with a temperate smile as she sees panic wash over his face.

Not knowing why, Miles suddenly feels relaxed with Sam's presence. He never thought he could fully trust another human being as he never had before in his entire life, but Sam seems to be able to stir up positive and warm feelings inside him.

With her simple smile, well, and the fact that she didn't kill him in his sleep, Miles feels as if he can now depend his survival on her. His previous thought of wanting to drop her off and feed her to the cannibals begins to rattle a sense of guilt within him.

"Yeah, I know," he responds, both fully knowing the implications.

"Good," she smiles harmoniously.

Taking a closer look at her, Miles notices something different about her face. She looks so, well, beautiful. Then he realizes why. She is clean, and she looks incredible when she's not covered in dirt and filth. He could feel a tingling sensation running through him, a sensation that he had only ever felt when he was in lust.

Sam's transformation from a nameless and sexless entity to a real woman is enough to make Miles forget why he ever doubted her in the first place.

Despite months alone in isolation, he still feels no real romantic attraction toward her. Not yet, anyway.

However, Miles can already see that she is a very attractive woman, and it isn't difficult to predict the effect she would have on him once she regains her strength.

With this thought emerging in his mind, he needs to get rid of her quick if he decides he wants to do it; once she is back on her feet, she may become difficult to destroy, or even worse, he may end up developing feelings for his nemesis.

"I'm thinking maybe we can venture out in a few days and search for some supplies," she speaks as Miles continues to stare at her.

"Do you know of a place? The town where I found you was completely run dry," Miles questions in disbelief.

"Tannersville. You made the mistake of tackling the towns during the day. At night, the infected all fall asleep, leaving the supplies untouched. But I know a place, Tannersville, if you trust me."

"Sounds risky," Miles answers, fully knowing he would follow her regardless as his attraction toward her slowly becomes stronger and stronger.

"It's okay. I know you're worried, but we can do this. We just need a little luck. That's your strength, not mine."

"Okay," Miles responds, thinking this is the gutsiest woman, no person, he has ever met, much more fearless than he is.

Nothing else needs to be said. They sit quietly on a log, side by side, watching the grey and gentle clouds pass through the still sky, each lost in their own thoughts.

———

Hours later, Miles finds himself back in the comfort and safety of his city condo, lounging on his sofa with his feet up on the coffee table and enjoying a cold beer, when he experiences a sudden feeling of soft lips pressing against his.

He opens his eyes to find that it was all just a dream, and he is still stuck in this nightmare of an apocalypse.

Though, he would have been slightly more disappointed without Sam's smooth body lying on top of him.

Hey, I could live with this, he thinks to himself as her lips continue to glide along his. *A pretty good deal given the shitty situation.*

"Wow, not that I'm complaining, but what was that for?" Miles asks in ecstasy and thirst after Sam pulls away from him.

"That was... I don't know. Do I need a reason?" She smiles vulnerably at him, batting her extended eyelashes.

"No, no, certainly not. Feel free to keep going if you want some more." Miles grins, praying he doesn't appear moronic.

"That was for you being you," she cryptically says.

Women... Me being me? The unanimous opinion in the past had been that I was a douchebag. Either I had changed, or she is into kissing imbeciles.

His train of thought is interrupted rather rudely by another soulful kiss, this one with full lips and a massage of the tongue.

Damn, I could get used to this. I could get used to this if I don't fuck things up by kicking her out. No, I can't get used to this. The temptation would surely suck me in.

They stare into each other's eyes and can feel the stirring lust again. They grab each other in such frenzy, kissing and moaning in ecstasy. They certainly can't get enough. They thirst and crave for each other. His lips continue to glide into hers, thrusting and pulling. Other times, it follows with a full kiss and a massage of the tongue.

It has been a long time since each of them felt like this toward anyone, and it excited them. A silver lining in a shitty situation. It is the only novelty the evening brought, but neither of them complained. They try it several more times, almost too many times, and they both loved it.

As it grows darker, she snuggles in his arms, and together, they watch the featureless and depressing room as it reminds them of their impending doom. It doesn't matter, though. They are together and happy.

————

The following night seeks to be the first they spend together, truly together, doing absolutely nothing but snuggle and kiss. For some reason, her nightmares of her secret past don't seem to haunt her as much anymore as long as she remains snuggled by his side.

Nonetheless, Miles is willing to make that sacrifice for this noble endeavor. Strangely, his own, admittedly much milder, nightmares have stopped as well since she entered his life.

He had planned for such a disaster. He had money, and he used it to isolate himself as best he could from the effects of humanity's self-destruction. He had bravely gotten away, physically unscathed with supplies intact.

With all that though, if it hadn't been for Sam, Miles would still be wandering aimlessly around Siberia, counting the days until he runs out of food and dies.

Perhaps, in some subconscious way, he had chosen that way to die. Not for him to die in the brilliant light of a nuclear holocaust, or to find himself on the losing side in a mafia war and bleed out in a street somewhere.

No, he would survive the catastrophe with his own wits, preparation, and money, only to hide in the middle of Siberia until death found him, a passive victim. Typical Miles, despite all his money and selfishness, he still could not save himself.

Miles took one proactive step in salvaging Sam, a decision

he had been regretting the past several days. Now, he is planning for a long-term future with her.

What has he become? Who has he become? That determined optimism of hers is contagious. Even more than that, she had given him a kick in the ass and a jump start into a whole different world he had been unknown to.

CHAPTER 10
IN SEARCH FOR FREEDOM

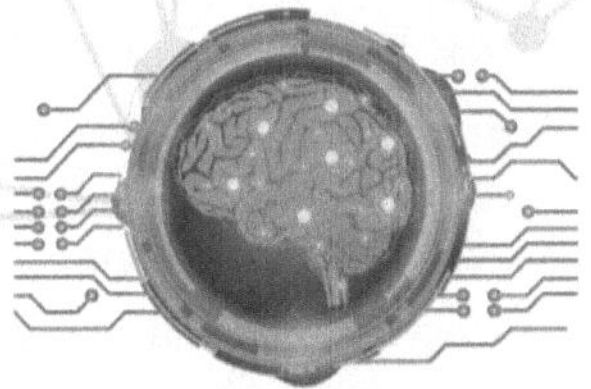

A FEW NIGHTS LATER, Sam and Miles find themselves trudging through thick snow toward Tannersville. Miles continues to shiver in the frigidity, with anxiety washing over him, while Sam remains calm.

He continues to wonder how she could remain so damn calm when they're both headed toward their terminations. Maybe having already survived hell had made her tougher, less worried about the future.

They remain uncommunicative as they approach the run-down town of Tannersville. She leads, as she knows the town much better than he does. There is no one to be seen anywhere.

Maybe she's right about the greatly decreased population density in Tannersville. Miles feels a great deal of sorrow and culpability for all who had died, but at that moment, he sees it as a saving grace as the competition for resources had been eliminated.

"It's that small building right over there," Sam points out as they approach the entrance of the town.

"Alright ba... I mean, Sam." Miles catches himself and smiles coyly to hide his embarrassment.

There is a time and place for romance, and this isn't it. He looks at her, and then it dawns on him that she hadn't noticed the costly mistake he just made. There is a fiery drive in her, a determination to accomplish their mission.

'Time to get shit done. Why not? Not like there's a whole lot waiting to get done today.' Miles reflects as he follows Sam's cautious steps around the bodies and traps.

Finally reaching the shop, Miles squints through the glass door to see if anyone is waiting for them inside. He couldn't see anyone, but that doesn't mean much; it's too dark to see even if there is a large crowd waiting inside. The shelves near the door appears to be mostly empty.

As expected, the shelves had already been torn down one by one by their predecessors in burglary. He looks around his surroundings several times before generating the nerve to enter the store.

But something feels wrong. Miles knows it, feels it. Someone is watching them. Miles begins to panic and looks back at Sam, who calmly alternates between checking her surroundings and trying to look inside the shop.

"Okay, you have the knife, and you're the man. Open the door and go in. I'll have your back with this stick," she finally speaks up with her own self-devised plan.

Did that sound like a plan? Fuck no! It sounded like suicide. We have no idea who or what is waiting inside this wretched place, and here she is telling me to go in first. Still, Sam is my woman now, and I'd have to protect her.

That's the moment Miles realizes he had never protected anybody or had been protected by anyone before. It didn't need to take a shitty situation for him to prove his love for her, but it needs to be done.

Wait, what? Love? Did I just think that? Anyway, time to open that damn door.

It creaks like a bitch even when he tries to open it silently. To his relief, nothing jumps out at him. He tentatively inches his way inside, his eyes blinding as they adjust to the dark and dust inside the store. He can hear noise coming from all directions around him but can't see a damn thing.

Cold fear courses through his body as he continues to stride with light steps. Just to do something, he takes out his knife and points in a random direction, stabbing air in attempts to impress Sam.

Like an idiot, he even makes some "huh" noises as a rat scuttles out of the door while Sam unsuccessfully tries to hide her nonstop giggling.

"Clearly, you were in some sort of special forces unit," Sam jokes from behind.

"Hey, don't mock me..." Miles tries to remain indignant before he starts to smile as well, his eyes adjusting to his surroundings as he searches around.

"Don't worry about it. I'll get what we need." Sam laughs a bit more, leaving Miles feeling weak and incapable.

Miles sees the shop littered with opened containers and small packages of rice. He grabs as many as he can hold and heads out the door.

"That's it. Let's get out of here, Sam."

They turn around to leave, realizing two things. One, they haven't checked their surroundings in a while and two, there is a burly man standing by the front door, nonchalantly watching them. He is wearing a blue bandana on his head, and Miles briefly wonders whether that is a gang symbol or just a terrible fashion statement.

The man is dressed in what might have been some kind of mechanic's overall during the medieval times, but is now just cloth hanging from him in a haphazard manner. He is clearly on the verge of starvation, looking so grey that Miles is afraid he would dissolve into dust at any moment. His panic finally turns into pity as he stares into the vacant, hollow eyes. This is a dead man walking.

Miles's pity evaporates as he slowly shakes his head as if to clear it. Frozen in place, Miles watches as the man closes in on them. There is dried blood mixed with rust along his dull blade. This would not be the man's first time. This man knows what he is doing. He begins to slowly wobble toward Miles, letting his outstretched arm and attached rusty knife lead the way. Time slows.

Miles has no idea what to do next. He doesn't have a clue about knife fights, already reaching the limit of his knowledge when he held his own knife by the wrong end. They stare into each other's eyes as the man continues to slowly progress toward Miles and Sam.

This unreal, but somehow frightening, scene quickly becomes rudely interrupted by the solid force of Sam's fist making blunt contact with the back of the man's skull.

The man tumbles to the ground surprisingly gracefully. Hearing his knife rattle on the floor takes Miles out of his stupor. He gives Sam a thumbs-up and tries to appear confident, like that had been his plan all along.

However, he isn't sure he had convinced her as she is busy picking up the rice and leaving the deteriorated store. Not wanting to be a total loser, Miles grabs two more bags and follows her.

As soon as they step out of the store, Miles is shocked to see nothing there as he had assumed more of the dead men would be outside awaiting them. But there are no gangs, no hungry hordes, no desperate individuals wanting to join or kill them. That guy had been alone.

Miles takes another look around and feels calm enough to take in the surroundings again. There are cars and buildings, what's left of them anyway, but the town is mostly deserted and abandoned. The grass and trees are all either dead or in the process of dying, a truly depressing site to behold.

"Coming?" Sam interrupts Miles's serenity, reminding him this is not the time to let his guard down as they need to quickly leave and head back to base camp.

Halfway home, Miles feels a light tap on his left shoulder. He turns around and sees Sam, expecting another kiss, but quickly realizes that she's pointing to the horde of about eight people heading toward them from a distance.

Although they are much slower, they are still closing in fast. Miles and Sam pick up the pace, but as Miles looks behind him, the horde is also doing the same. Shit. This is going to be a tight race.

Miles watches helplessly as one of those anti-human monstrosities inches closer and closer. Fortunately for Miles, the miscreation is greeted by Sam's outstretched arm, with a knife awaiting him at the end. His own inertia drives the knife into his chest, black sludge gushing out as he falls to the ground.

Sam had assumed a wide stance, but it still surprises Miles to see her remain standing. She has more strength than he had thought, much more than he ever would.

The fallen man looks up at Sam, confused, as if he had this one important question right at the tip of his tongue but can no longer remember what it was. He opens his mouth and points at her as if beginning a conversation, but all that comes out of his mouth is more sludge, leaving Sam still standing with her knife, towering the man as he clutches his chest and disintegrates.

Holy crap, that was impressive, Miles thinks as he gawks at the brute strength of his new girl.

She had just killed a guy, protecting the both of them, something Miles is not even sure he could have done.

While he is still admiring her determination and skill, it occurs to him that she really could easily kill him whenever she chooses. She has the toughness Miles lacks, toughness that could not be developed with money and pure solitude.

We did it. We risked a lot, but we also gained some, though not as much. Sure, we now have more food; that is a success that could not be denied. Life for us could have been even better if we were able to find some sort of protein to keep our strengths, but that hadn't happened. I guess Sam feels guilty for risking their lives just for some measly bags of rice, killing unnecessary humans just to survive.

The way I see it, if it hadn't been for her, I would surely be dead right now. However, the most important part of this trip isn't even the kills on our hands; it is the bond we created in the process. We are a real team now, Miles reflects on the moment they shared, fully trusting himself in Sam as their teamwork makes him almost euphoric.

CHAPTER 11
LASACTKA CREATOR REVEALED

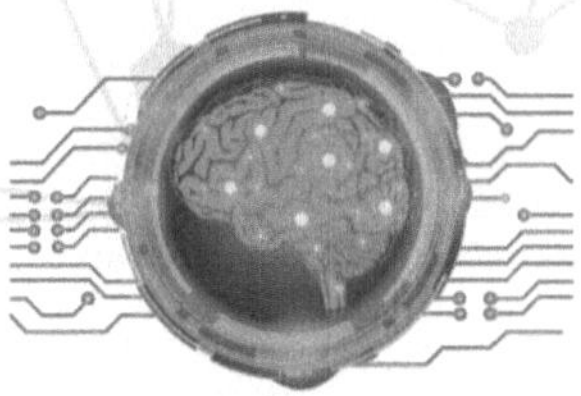

One luminous morning, while Sam is out enjoying the sun, Miles goes over to her blanket to fold the mess she had made.

I love her, but man, she is a slob, he thinks.

He picks up her thin wool blanket from the ground, and a small book falls out, almost like a journal. Miles knows he shouldn't read it, but he is too curious to put it down.

Maybe it's her diary. Maybe it's about him, her secret thoughts and feelings toward him. His curiosity overpowers his conscience, and he opens her supposed diary.

Surprisingly, in it are documentations, experiment-like

writings dating back to over a decade ago. What the hell is this?

PROPERTY OF SAMANTHA MARE. DEDICATED PROTÉGÉ OF DR. JAMES FARROW.

Miles begins reading the extremely dense book filled with information on Lasactka, information unknown to public knowledge, dating back to when Samantha first helped isolate the virus from the brain of a yak.

The more he reads, the more he discovers that she is actually the creator of this deadly virus that wiped out humanity and human intelligence.

The Lasactka virus was supposed to save the human race by increasing their intelligence and giving them unlimited knowledge to accomplish anything. Instead, the virus had reversed the brain capacity of all humans to the size of a mere pea and turned everyone stupid and incompetent.

No. It can't be. Not my Sam, Miles ponders in disbelief.

He questions her when she returns from her morning walk and rather than denying it, she immediately breaks down into tears as she falls to the ground.

"I knew you wouldn't understand if I told you. That's why I wanted to kill myself that day we met. I had destroyed the world. It's all my fault. I should have stopped him. Dr. Farrow. I should have known all along that he didn't want this virus created to promote humanity; he wanted this virus created to get revenge on all those who had made fun of him for his elaborate inventions.

I should have known. I'm so stupid. I should have known better than to blindly listen to everything he told me. 'Just trust me,' he'd say when I questioned his procedures. But he kept reassuring me that he knew what he was doing so I just went along with it. He played me for a fool, used me as a scapegoat for taking responsibility of Lasactka while he fled, getting what he wanted but never having to own up to it.

I promoted this virus to people. I was so proud of what we

had done that I stood by it. However, weeks after it was released, I saw people around me getting dumber and dumber. The city stopped functioning, and the world entered a mass homicide and suicide brigade. I'm sorry I didn't tell you. You would've kicked me out if I did," Sam continues to plead as her entire confession spills out.

She isn't wrong. If I hadn't gotten close to her, I would've murdered her on the spot for taking my life away from me. What the hell is wrong with this woman? How could she be a scientist, a doctor even, and not realize that she was releasing a deadly virus into the world? And to remain so proud of it? God, she is an idiot! Miles thinks to himself, becoming angrier with each word Sam speaks.

"You think I'm stupid, don't you?" Sam asks, her voice trembling.

Of course, I do! You fucking destroyed the world! Miles wants to scream, but instead, tries to remain still and collected. "No, you got screwed over. It wasn't necessarily your fault."

Miles could see tears beginning to flow down her eyes. Maybe she really isn't at fault for the demise of the world. After all, she had been tricked because she was just like the rest of the world, incompetent.

"Is there a cure? You created it. There has to be a cure, right?"

Still in tears, Sam looks up at Miles like a sad little puppy.

"I don't know. I don't know! I spent months trying to find one. I crossed every species I could possibly think of to combat the mutating virus strain, but each time I tried, the virus only grew stronger while the population of the people grew weaker.

When this virus was first released, it progressed slowly, making us think that it was actually benefiting mankind. However, the virus multiplied and mutated at an exponential rate, quickly spreading throughout the human brains and causing everyone to behave oblivious and uneducated."

"There has to be something you can do. Something! I had family who fell victim to this fucked-up bug. Do something!"

By this point, Miles no longer cares that Sam and him had something intimate. She clearly had given up hope and didn't seem to care about saving the world. Miles doesn't know if she was stupid before the virus or if she is just infected, but something must be done.

"This Dr. Farrow. You said it was his idea? His old fucked-up mind created this fucked-up thing? Where is he now?"

"I don't know. As soon as the virus was isolated, he just disappeared one day, leaving a note that said not to look for him."

"You don't have his number? Email? Address? Anything!?"

"I met Dr. Farrow in the middle of the Himalayan mountains. Everything he had was outdated. We were only able to communicate with each other because I lived in the mountains with him for over six years. After I found out the true purpose of Lasactka, I burned down his lab, fearful of what else would rise from it if I didn't."

"So, what now? You're just going to give up? Let all these people die from their own stupidity?"

"I don't have any other choice. It's too late!"

Miles now becomes very angry. He loved this woman, and it turns out that she's nothing but a heartless piece of shit.

Without saying another word, he grabs his bag, throws some cans of beans and a small bag of rice into it, and storms out the shelter.

He hates Sam, but he still has to leave some food behind for her; he refuses to stoop to her level. He could not become as heartless as her. His conscience would destroy him if he leaves her there to starve. At least she is warm and safe from the cold, unlike him. Miles has to brace himself for the frigid wind that awaits him behind those closed doors.

CHAPTER 12
THE FINAL STRAW

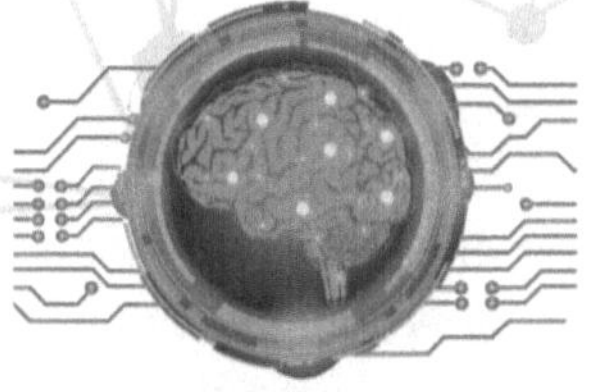

HERE HE IS, back out in the cold. It feels like it was just last week that he had walked through this same frigid cold to his shelter, the shelter that was supposed to be his saving grace but has now become his enemy.

What now? I can't stay out in the cold. The wind would send me to my death within days. I can't go back to my shelter. The sight of Sam makes me want to put my knife in her throat. There is only one thing left to do. I have to find this Dr. Farrow and get him to reverse this virus with whatever it takes.

But Miles has no lead. He doesn't even know the first

name of this doctor or whether he's even still alive. The only information Sam had given him was that he has a laboratory in the heart of the Himalayas, or had, at least. Planes are no longer in service, for obvious reasons. Even if they are, Miles wouldn't feel safe getting on one as he'd die before the plane even reached the sky.

And with his car shredded into pieces and turned into a playground for retired lawyers, his only option is to walk to the Himalayan mountains. His feet are already frozen, and he doesn't know how much further his shoes would be able to take him.

Still, he has to try. He can keep telling himself that he needs to do this to save the world, but truth is, he is really just trying to go big to clear his conscience for sleeping with the enemy and leaving those back home to rot when he could have saved them. Even if Miles dies before he gets there, at least his conscience would be cleared.

Over the next few weeks, he continues to trudge through mountains of snow. Hell, Miles isn't even really sure if he's heading in the right direction. He has a tricked-out compass and a poor sense of direction. He figures he'd keep heading south until he sees some epic mountains.

Looking back, he regrets not paying attention in geography class. That way, he could at least get a sense of direction as to how far this place actually is. His best guess is a solid 100 miles. 100 miles. Shit. No way is he ever going to make that.

Miles clips his bag around his waist to secure it around his body. He then crunches on a handful of beans, now frozen as ice, psyching himself for the journey. With his estimate, he should be able to get there in under a week if he keeps a steady pace.

As he continues walking, the land that used to thrive with modern technology and prospering success has now turned to crumbling debris, and accomplished hopefuls have now turned to toddlers. It was just a short two months ago when Miles was offered the chance to become a part of Mensa.

Now, that society no longer means anything other than five letters on a piece of paper.

His entire life, he had worked diligently to get to where he is, intellectual, studious, and determined. Now, he's marching toward his death with no hopes of surviving his journey.

What was all that even for? What's the point of trying in the first place, wasting my life, if all that resulted is chaos and the downfall of society? It just goes to show that everything is indeed only temporary. I wish I had dedicated my life to learning more valuable and useful information, like how the bloody hell I'm going to get to the Himalayas rather than learning about the life of the Greek Gods. Thirty years. Thirty years I have wasted on useless knowledge. Thirty. Fucking. Years.

———

Approximately a week later, Miles finds himself still on barren grounds with views of mountains nowhere in sight. He continues trekking several more miles until he finds himself face to face with a sign: WELCOME TO VILYUYSK, RUSSIA.

Russia? No, no, no. It can't be. I should be a lot closer to Nepal by now. Not Russia. Miles looks down at his feet. Frostbite had claimed several of his toes in the frigid cold, and his skin begins to bleed from all the cracks and splits. *That's it. It's over. I can't continue. I can't continue my search for Dr. Farrow to try to end this nightmare. I can't save the world.*

Miles's legs buckle, and his feet turn numb with paralysis. He sees a desolate town in the near distance and proceeds to pull himself toward it, legs dragging behind him in the snow. This vibrant town used to be full of cheerful hopefuls and wise elders who have now turned into clueless zombies, colliding into cars and engaging in nonsensical conversations.

He ignores them and continues trailing. When the infection first started, he used to run away while blowing their faces off, hoping the infection didn't spread to him. But now, it no longer matters. He is already infected. He is already one of them. It is just a matter of time before he turns too.

Miles has no idea where he's walking or even going. He just feels the need to keep going even though he is fully aware he would never make it to his destination. Eventually, Miles's legs give out, and he collapses onto the ground, his forehead whacking against the concrete.

Out of the corner of his right eye, he spots one of the only buildings remaining in this town that has not been completely destroyed by the infected. Miles limps over and finds a metal sign that must have fallen off the front: PRYLER INTELLIGENCE.

He had heard of this company before. Long before Lasactka destroyed all intelligence and human brains, Pryler Intelligence was a social media corporation that helped people boost their online presence and status with their new app: Pry.

People had been so obsessed with increasing the credibility of their social media presence that their desperation had driven the motivation and creation of Pry.

Pryler Intelligence created an app that scanned the life of each person who signed up and completed a questionnaire of the life they wished they could live. Pry then created constructed images and captions that helped people showcase their "desired lives" and "best selves" without ever having to lift a single finger.

Pry offered people the opportunity to gain all the fame while doing none of the work. No longer did people have to ponder on the best words to say to capture the "perfect" moments. No longer did people have to perform endless research on how to beat out the competition.

With Pry, people were able to propel up the social media

chain, showcasing their greatest wishes as reality while they actually did nothing.

Miles picks up the sign and tosses it onto the bleak street. Even a company like Pryler, one of the corporations in this world with the greatest inventions, had fallen victim to this virus.

Miles walks into the building through the half-detached doors and finds himself facing dozens upon dozens of smashed computers and whiteboards, adorned with a fucked-up game of Hangman. He tries switching on the light, but both the power and heat had been out for months. Great.

He continues roaming through the offices, where apps like "Pry" had been created, that have now all turned to storage for blanket forts.

"Well, at least it's better than nothing," he sighs as he takes shelter beneath one of the burlap-designed forts.

Miles reaches into his bag and pulls out Sam's journal. He was going to use this journal to jog Dr. Farrow's memory. It was more than likely that the doctor had forgotten exactly what went into making the virus. Miles cracks his bleeding knuckles. He would have been able to make the doctor remember, no matter what it took.

He gazes at his bleeding hands and the journal once more. None of it matters anymore. His hopes of making it to the laboratory have gone to dust. With all hopes lost, Miles flips open to a blank page and begins to write.

To those who find this, I'm sorry. I tried to stop it. I tried to stop Lasactka. I kept using the excuse of this trip as a way to relieve myself of the guilt, but I had so many chances to stop Lasactka from happening. I saw it coming.

I had predicted the impending end of the world sooner than it had actually happened, but I did nothing to stop it. I guess there's no need to hold in this secret any longer. I knew Samantha and Dr. Farrow.

I'm surprised she didn't recognize me, but I was on the plane with her in Lukla when it crashed. I thought I was the only survivor when I suddenly saw a weak girl push part of the aircraft wing off and stumble toward the mountains. I didn't know who she was or where she was going, but I followed her anyway, always maintaining a safe distance behind.

Sure, I could have helped her, but I didn't want to frighten her. I was there when she had the conversation with Dr. Farrow and when he introduced his concept of the Lasactka virus to her. I tried to remain discrete, but I foolishly tripped over a rock and fell flat on my face before them, causing them to notice me and pull me into their lab as their test subject.

I am patient zero.

I saw through months of trials, being forcibly injected several strains of viruses each time. After about three weeks into their experimentation, I was no longer able to think clearly. Then the final strain of Lasactka was ready.

They promised me that this virus would surely work. I didn't believe them. I knew there were going to be complications. I even laughed in their faces. But despite my thoughts, there was nothing I could have done.

They injected the virus into my temple, and my eyes began to blur. It almost felt like I was hallucinating as I faced a short period where I didn't even know where I was. I could have stopped them.

While I was tripped out, I overheard Dr. Farrow telling his assistant, Penlay, his true plans with the virus. If I hadn't been so high, I might have been able to remember to spread the word when I finally escaped... twelve months too late.

To this day, I don't know why Lasactka didn't turn me as quickly as it turned those around me when it went airborne. Perhaps the strain I was injected with was a milder form.

All I know is, I am infected, and I am destined to turn. I'm sorry everyone for destroying you. I'm sorry for being so stupid. I'm sorry for being so... oo... oo...

Miles suddenly becomes distracted and drops the pen and journal. He sees a torn electrical wire and walks toward it.

"Shiny... I need to touch. I need to touch now," he says as he inches closer toward the wire. "Fruity Twizzlers?"

With that, he grabs the wires, puts them in his mouth, and chews.

And everything turns dark.

We are all victims of modern society. We all want something more, something we know we can never achieve. And when we finally do, we perish to our own selfish ignorance.

JUST LIKE ME
FALLEN VICTIMS OF THE MIND

Fatalities of the Modern World Book Two

PROLOGUE

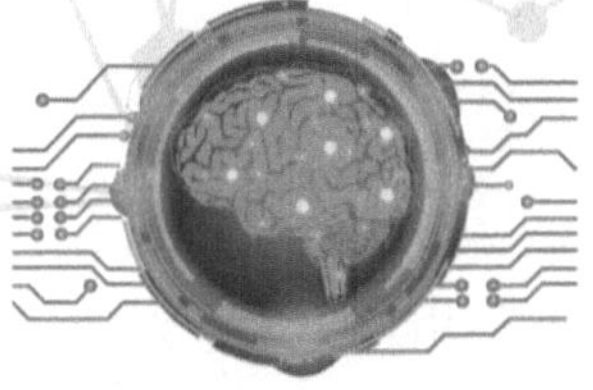

THE HUMAN MIND is extremely malleable, capable of constantly changing ideas and beliefs based on current wants and desires, driven by emotions and vain.

We think we know what we want at any given time. We tell ourselves that we are strong and capable enough to stand by our beliefs and moral concepts, but most of us only do it for show. When opportunity comes up for us to disregard those "core beliefs," we allow it to happen.

As vulnerable human beings, we always believe that the "thing" we do not have is the "thing" that will make our lives complete and our satisfactions whole. We constantly chase after these "things" that others seem to have and automatically correlate them with life happiness.

However, what we continuously fail to realize is that our individual beings are what gives us the most satisfaction, long term that is.

What happens when we can finally afford that new purse that everyone swears "makes their life complete"? What happens when we finally get our hands on that new phone that everyone promises will "provide life-long happiness"?

What happens when we finally reach one million followers on Instagram and receive as many as 5,000 likes and comments per day? Will that give us satisfaction that lies beyond skin-deep? What happens when we finally wake up one morning with the face and body of a model or a celebrity? Will that give us happiness and self-approval that is not only reflected in a mirror?

Think about it. We spend all this time and energy WISHING we could be like someone else, WISHING we have the "things" that others have, and BELIEVING that our lives would be ten times better than they are now if we can just obtain those "things."

These "things," however, are only distractions from a greater issue, a greater issue that lies beneath us, where we obliviously believe that true bliss and fulfillment within ourselves can come from obtaining external objects and replacing the appearance of who we are with the appearance of someone else.

But how can we replace something that's internal with external materials? How can we create inner contentment with external substances? If we obtain that "thing" we crave for so much, won't another "thing" come along at another point in time and make us yearn for that new "thing"?

What if we had the face of the supermodel we are currently envious of? Won't a new supermodel, with a different face, come along and make us wish we could look like the latter?

Transient materials can never provide us with true gratification if we don't know what we are looking for. We never take the time to reflect on what makes us who we are, constantly trying to replace who we are before giving us a chance to figure it out.

We relentlessly believe that we will never have enough or that we will never be good enough because we don't have set goals or expectations. Our beliefs are always changing, based on feelings, based on societal pressure, or based on the need to belong.

We believe that having a different face and appearance will make us more likeable, and therefore, more content with ourselves when we are isolated from partners and social groups. However, this strong desire fades when we feel welcomed and accepted by those we crave acceptance from.

We believe that gaining fame through social media and becoming a well-known influencer will drive greater gratification in us toward life when those around us criticize us as being "no one" or "nothing" otherwise.

We believe that if everyone around us likes us then, eventually, we will learn to like ourselves. However, without this pressure driving us toward reaching fame and glory, our thoughts and desires may be completely different.

We believe that obtaining that new phone or that new purse will make us feel like we belong in certain social groups because society has told us that certain social groups are the "best ones," and if we are not in them, we do not have value.

Even if we have previously opposed or loathed the "popular" social groups, we give into the pressure when we feel we are being left out.

The constant need to be what everyone else is or to have what everyone else has only makes us miss out on the qualities that make us human.

The endless mission we have in searching for what we don't have only causes us to miss out on what we do have, eventually triggering us to completely forget why we even began that mission, leaving us to blindly follow what we no longer understand.

CHAPTER 1

THE WIND BLOWS. The crows caw. The rain pours.

One sits on a wooden bench, secluded in the middle of a dark forest underneath the gloomy clouds, gazing deeply into Two's eyes.

It is the year 2065 and the forest is desolate, but the sounds of the blaring city of Lustville can still be heard from a distance. The forest is adorned with web-covered tombstones, scattered chaotically throughout the land, and non-flowering green bushes, sprawled across the perimeter of the woods.

There are a couple of abandoned trucks and cars for sexually-charged teens and adulterers, along with a few half-buried bodies lying beneath the soil, but other than that, the forest is mostly covered with dead grass and crumbling rocks.

It is a frigid winter afternoon, with a thunderstorm brewing behind the threatening clouds, embracing the entire town in its pertinent darkness. One's silver white hair covers his head, with his bangs hanging over the left side of his face, hiding his expression of indifference.

Two sits, submissively, across from him, with her long curly silver white hair flowing in the strong wind, gusting locks of hair across her perfectly oval face, embellished with dark brown eyes and thin painted lips.

Two stares back at One, seemingly timid and shy, and smiles.

"Two." One says, holding onto her small hands. "I think we should get married."

Two shifts, uncomfortably, while adjusting her long silver dress.

"I think so too." Two replies. "But what about your relationship with Three?"

"That can still continue. Three is aware of my relationship with you. Besides, I'll get tired of her soon enough anyway. You can also have your own side relationship. I've been waiting for you to get one."

"Hmm, well I do have Four. But, won't Three have a problem with you marrying me? Don't you want her more?"

"Why would she have a problem? She knows she's nothing more to me than an affair. Besides, she would never leave her husband for me. You and I have better chemistry than me and her, or even you and Four. You know that."

"I suppose you're right. Okay, I'll marry you!"

As soon as Two finishes her sentence, One reaches into his pocket, pulling out a small and red velvet box. He opens it, revealing the most stunning ring embedded in amethyst lining. The ring has a diamond stone, shining magnificently even in the midst of gloomy dusk.

One slips it onto Two's already held out ring finger, over the tan line of her previous ring, and they kiss. They are now engaged to be married.

Watching this, through binoculars, from a latticed apartment window facing the forest, is Five. Five's modern apartment building complex is sixteen stories high, overlooking the town of Lustville and painted a beautiful hue of silver.

Standing inside her twelfth-floor apartment, she peers out into the woods with a blank expression on her face.

Her living room is decorated with silver antique pieces of furniture she bought from multiple thrift stores. There are two old-fashioned light silver velvet armchairs in the middle of the room.

Five's oldest friend sits on one of the chairs, sipping a cup of pumpkin spice latte and crunching on kale chips.

She looks like Five, with neatly curled long silver white hair hanging loosely down her back and a single strand of her bangs decorating her structured face. Five is wearing a long and flowing silver dress while her friend is wearing the same.

After staring absent-mindedly and indifferently at both Two and One for over an hour, Five walks away from the window, staring at the ring on her finger and running her thumb over an engraving that says, "One Loves Five Forever," without a single emotion drawn on her face.

She cannot remember why this ring is on her finger. She cannot recall whether this ring means something or who One is, for that matter. She only assumes that this ring is one of the many she had stolen from her friends over the years.

She sits back down, placing herself gently on the light silver armchair across from her friend.

"Well, Six, it's been a while since we saw each other. What do you want?" Five interrogates, calmly.

"No reason. I was just in the neighborhood and wanted to stop by to see my good friend."

Her friend, Six, replies, taking another sip of her pumpkin spice latte.

"Six, we haven't seen or spoken to each other in years. I barely recognized you when you rang my doorbell. Now, tell me, why are you here?"

"Alright, fine, fine. You caught me. I just need to borrow some money. I've been struggling to make ends meet since my husband passed away. The little I get from the government is barely enough to cover my basic expenses like food and rent."

Six grins, wickedly, as Five turns around to pick up her cup of pumpkin spice latte.

"Well, MY HUSBAND is extremely wealthy, bringing in more money than we could ever spend. We are, in fact, on our way to becoming millionaires. Of course, I can spare you some chump change." Five laughs, boastfully.

With this, she gets up from her seat and walks off, with perfect and petite steps, into her bedroom. Barely a minute later, she returns with a wad of cash in her hand.

"Here you go. Two thousand dollars. That should be more than enough. Now get out of here, you filthy hobo." Five says, tossing the money at Six, bills scattering across her silver carpet.

Six beams at Five as she gets down on her knees to pick up the money.

"Thank you, Five. Thank you! I owe you one. You're the best!" Six replies, picking her small silver purse up from the floor as she stands up and walks out the front door.

Back in her own apartment, the most expensive luxury condominium in the city, Six walks into her bedroom, painted royal silver with gold embellishments, and tosses her cheap and old purse into a hamper labeled "Props."

On one side of her room stands a tall shelf, lined with

numerous name-brand and luxury purses. She lightly touches one adorned with gold diamonds and chuckles to herself.

"I can't believe that idiot was stupid enough to buy my story. No wonder we're no longer friends." Six laughs, roguishly, as she surrounds herself with thousands of purses she had bought with the money she got from scamming people.

CHAPTER 2

THE CITY TREMBLES as the towering bell rings. Work has ended, and the streets become packed with hordes of men rushing into their silver cars and speeding to get home, disregarding the dozens of deaths and accidents they cause every day in the process.

Men dressed in silver dress shirts and silver tailored pants line the streets as they cross each other with simultaneous steps and huge grins decorating their faces. The men all smile at each other, saying "hello," with obvious fallacy, as if they are on auto-pilot.

Seven stands in front of his work building. Seven is a small fellow, with a balding silver white hairline and brown eyes. Seven has just been laid off from his job for shooting the CEO of his company, smiling and grinning despite the horrible situation.

He scans the crowd around him for his prey, watching men robotically walk by him, one by one. Out of the corner of his eye, he sees a tall and thin man, dressed in a silver dress shirt and silver tailored pants, cross the street.

Seven had stolen from others in the past, during the many other times he had lost his job, and because he is far from being a professional, his method of action is usually to resort to physical violence.

Seven is small and stout, but violence and physical blows come naturally to him. He has been training, learning to fight and wrestle, for the past five years.

Confidently, Seven comes up behind the man, grabs him by the collar, and yanks the man to the ground. The man falls, taken aback by the sudden attack. People surrounding them begin to form a crowd, entertaining themselves by cheering and betting money on who will be victorious.

Seven has full control over the man, driving a wrenching punch into the man's abdomen. The man doubles over in pain, waving his hands up as a sign of forfeiture, allowing Seven to steal his wallet, his keys, and his car.

The crowd around them continues to cheer and clap for Seven, without noticing or caring that they had just witnessed assault and theft. Seven slowly drives away, unaware and unconcerned that the man he had just fought is bleeding to his death.

Watching this scene unfold, in the luxury of her sleek silver car, parked along the sidewalk in front of a regal jewelry store called "The Glam," is Eight.

Eight had been traveling around the world for the past six months, shopping in cities like Milaxa and Pasira, and lying on beaches in islands like the Malvyves and Seychyllix. She stopped when she heard the commotion on her way back home.

She had watched the fight with indifference. Like all the others, she does not see a problem in what had happened. She sees fights like this almost every day as part of her normal routine, almost as if she is watching television.

Glancing around the streets, Eight notices a few local bookstores advertising her latest book, "Be Your Best You," a self-help and psychological novel teaching young women how to channel their own unique personalities, accept their flaws, and become aware of their own moral conscience.

Eight feels proud of herself as she sees a group of young women, all dressed in long silver dresses, gawking at her book through the store windows.

Everybody in town knows Eight. She is a local celebrity. She cannot remember her life prior to becoming famous five years ago, prior to having one of her social media posts on a popular platform called "BLykeMe," where she stands at a rally protesting about how women deserve be different and independent, along with hundreds of other women dressed in long silver dresses, go viral, and propel her into fame.

Everyone in town loves posting about their life on BLykeMe, as it is the only social media platform that allows people to share openly and honestly without consequences or judgments.

Women in Lustville do not have professional careers. They thrive on their husbands taking care of them and giving them the money they want to buy themselves expensive presents and gifts.

Lustville is no ordinary town. In Lustville, individual differences do not exist. Everyone is the same. Everyone looks the same.

Everyone dresses the same. Everyone behaves the same. Everyone is a clone of the person sitting or standing next to him or her. In this town, unique thoughts and unique opinions do not exist. Personalities do not exist. No one is able to explain their own identities because no one has an identity.

There are no names, no individual minds, no souls. However, because of this, no one is able to fault another person for their sins. No one is able to generate feelings of anger or envy toward another because there are no longer reasons to.

No one is able to generate emotions at all, only mimicking gestures that they have been taught and programmed to have, with no true understanding of why they are creating such gestures.

Everyone is free to do whatever they want, no consequences, no blame, no morals. Everyone is a branch off the same dysfunctional tree.

CHAPTER 3

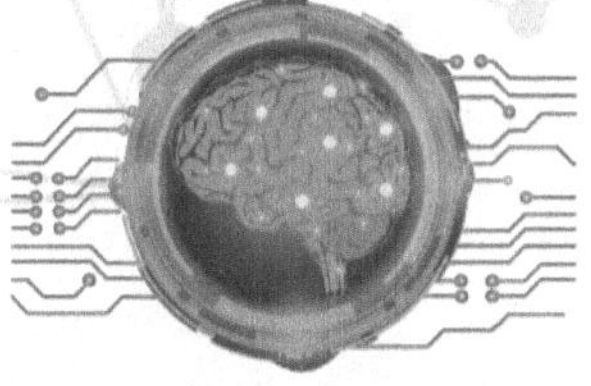

"RING!" The cacophonous alarm sounds, alarming the songbirds as they fly off the windowsill of Fourteen's apartment and into the fierce wind.

It is a cold winter morning, with the bright sun shining behind the thick overcast clouds. Rain had slowly been trickling down from the dark sky for the past seven hours.

Startled, Fourteen jumps up from her soft bed, covered with silver decorated pillows and silver polyester sheets. She had just been dreaming about her sweet and sane life back home, where people are different yet proud of it.

Instead, she wakes up to the soulless life she is living now, a life on auto-pilot, unable to do or say as she pleases or else she risks getting killed.

Fourteen is not a morning person, as she yawns and wipes the drool off her chin. Her alarm had surprised her so much that she almost fell out of bed, which she had done once or twice, or ten times, before. She opens her eyes to an eerily quiet morning, as she usually does.

She does not know how she can predict it, but eerily quiet mornings are usually a warning that someone is about to die. Back home, this used to surprise people. People used to come from all over the world and awe at her premonitions. Some even feared her as they thought being closer to her meant a higher chance of dying.

However, in Lustville, where death happens so often, no one seems to care about her premonitions. Every quiet morning for her is met with fear and anxiety, with full knowledge that death is going to surround her and there is nothing she can do about it.

She shakes her head to get the fear out of her mind. There is never enough time in the mornings to worry about anything as she must present herself to her husband under gift wrap and bow (not literally, of course).

She hears the water running in the shower.

"Nine must be getting ready for work. I need to hurry!" Fourteen exclaims, as she quickly climbs out of bed and runs over to her vanity.

Her old vanity was decorated with photos of her travel experiences and the fun times she had with her friends back home. This new vanity, however, must remain a plain silver color so Fourteen would not accidentally get emotional over looking at a picture of her old life, especially in front of her husband.

Since only programmed emotions are allowed in Lustville, Fourteen has to carefully select the emotions she portrays in public. Whenever she feels an emotion that is "not programmed," she forces herself to wear a mask just to cover up her face.

Experiencing emotions that are not part of protocol causes the chip to beep, and since she doesn't have a chip, Fourteen must take caution to avoid getting caught and hung over the infamous bridge of Lustville, where all the bodies of "sinners" remain for eternity.

At her vanity, Fourteen rummages through boxes upon boxes of makeup that her husband had bought for her over the past few months. She normally doesn't wear makeup but, again, dressing up faces like clowns is one of the requirements of this world.

She grabs some powder and mascara, and she slaps them on her face to pretty herself up. There is a certain look that women in Lustville must wear. Eyelashes must be dark and thick. Eyebrows must be full and silver white. Lipstick must be adorned with a gentle brush of gloss.

Eyeliner and eyeshadow must always be different shades of black, and contouring is a must. Fourteen never even knew what contouring was before coming to Lustville.

"What's the point of creating fake lines on your body? It's barbaric! You either have it or you don't!" She quietly mumbles to herself every morning as she covers her face like a clown queen and pops a stick of gum into her mouth.

Gum. That's another thing. Gum is not allowed in Lustville because it has the potential of getting caught in someone's hair and ruining it. Anything that can accidentally ruin the appearance of Lustville and cause people to look different from one another is banned.

Fourteen is addicted to gum. She chews it whenever she gets nervous, and in a world where she must pretend to be someone she despises every second of the day, chewing gum seems to be the only thing keeping her sane.

Before she left, she had stashed her suitcase with packs

and packs of gum. Luckily, the security in Lustville cared more about what was in Fourteen's head than what was in her luggage.

Despite not seeing any use in adorning her face to look like a Halloween mask, she continues to every morning despite her opposing thoughts. Nine is not allowed to see her without a face of makeup on.

It is an unwritten rule that she must look "her best" for Nine whenever he sees her. She is only allowed to sleep after he sleeps so she could wash her makeup off, and she must sleep facing the opposite direction of Nine so he doesn't see her "disturbing" face in the mornings.

Thirty minutes of struggling with a blush brush and concealer later, she hurries into her closet, pulls out her long silver dress from the day before, hoping it doesn't smell as she had forgotten to do laundry, and draws it over her head, brushing it off as it flows to the ground.

Every morning is the same. Every morning needs to be the same. Every morning, Fourteen must be ready, perfectly pressed and groomed by the time Nine steps out of the shower.

She hears the shower turn off as the water drips.

"Shit!" Fourteen whispers to herself, bolting out of her closet.

Nine spends exactly eighteen minutes in the bathroom every morning after he turns the shower off. However, Fourteen must be ready and prepared the minute he turns the water off if he ever decides to step out earlier.

Seven minutes go by, and Nine is still in the bathroom. Fourteen can hear him still drying off his silver white locks. Nine loves to admire himself in the mirror whenever he steps foot into the bathroom, flexing his biceps and gleaming at his pecks and rock-hard abs.

"Shit!" Fourteen whispers to herself again, as she realizes that she is still chewing her gum.

She spits it out onto her left palm and reaches under her dress to hide it. She makes sure to secure her gum inside her underwear so it doesn't accidentally slip out in front of Nine. Nine has a zero-tolerance policy when it comes to chewing gum. If he ever caught her doing so, he would have no problem shooting her on the spot.

Last month, Nine found a gum wrapper in Fourteen's purse while he was looking for a pencil. Pencils are the only writing tools allowed in Lustville as pencil marks can be erased, making the canvas clean again without any unneeded permanent damage.

Fourteen likes to associate the erasing attribute of pencils with the clean slate in Lustville. No one has memories. No one has imperfections. No one has lives.

Nine almost beat Fourteen to death after he found the wrapper in her purse, only sparing her after she thoroughly explained to him that she bought the wrapper from a store called "The Other World" because she was curious as to what they looked like. She swore to him that she had no idea what and how gum even tastes like!

Even so, even if Nine does pound her to death, it would not matter as no one would care. Everyone in town would just praise Nine for his blunt strength and tenacity.

Eighteen minutes on the dot, Nine finally comes out of the bathroom, the bathroom filling up with steam and a strong scent of cologne behind him. He walks straight pass Fourteen without acknowledging her or even looking her way, leaving Fourteen standing there, smiling obnoxiously without breaking character.

This is no surprise. Nine never looks toward her way in the mornings. Ever since he "claimed" her, his interest in her has dwindled more and more. He spends more time with other women, constantly bringing them home while ignoring Fourteen.

However, Fourteen continues to dress up in her "daily

routine" because if she does not look picture perfect for her husband, consequences would be dire. She does not know what the consequences would be, but she doesn't want to find out.

In fact, Nine rarely ever speaks to Fourteen. They are married, but they do not love each other. How could they when love in Lustville is nonexistent? Before moving to Lustville, Fourteen had a fiancé, named Elijah, whom she loved. They were together for over ten years and spent every moment of every day together.

Sadly, five years ago, he committed suicide when his application for the "Hot & Young Fashion Influencer Program" was rejected, and the program selected men who were much brooder and richer than him.

Becoming a fashion influencer had always been Elijah's dream. They did not have a lot of money, so he had created his entire collection and style based on thrift store clothing and charitable donations. His social media page was extremely popular among the lower class, but the upper class always had the final say in who became the next "big thing."

After his death, Fourteen became extremely depressed and wanted to run away. She could no longer handle living inside her home, surrounded by constant reminders that her fiancé is no longer alive. She knew about the development of the chip and Lustville.

She saw it as the perfect chance to escape reality and live a fresh life on a blank slate. She hastily threw some of her belongings inside her suitcase, bracing herself for the new lifestyle she was about to endure, and hopped on the last plane flying out to Lustville.

However, what she didn't realize back then, is that life in Lustville is far different than the life she had envisioned, far worse than the life she had lived back home.

Upon arrival, she was screened and given a set of questions to ensure that she was indeed "one of them" and that she would not rebel. Everyone who enters Lustville is required to have a chip inside their brain and answer "yes" to every question asked.

Fourteen does not have the chip in her brain, but she was able to get past security because she had helped develop the chip and knew how to get around the requirements of entering the "new world."

On her second day in Lustville, Fourteen met Nine while walking across the streets after struggling for over an hour getting into her new "uniform."

Nine is a tall brooding man who wanted her and refused to take "no" for an answer. He continued to pester and follow her until she agreed to sleep with him, engaging in matrimony with him a few short months later.

Attempting to blend in with the common crowd in her new society, Fourteen agreed to marry Nine, despite how much she found Nine repulsive and still missed Elijah. It is much easier to pretend like she belongs in Lustville when she agrees, so her strong and forceful opinions would not accidentally shine through and give her away.

After Nine leaves their apartment for work, Fourteen quickly erases the dumb smile off her face, takes her gum out of her underwear, and hides it in her suitcase with hundreds of her other chewed up gum. She cannot risk flushing the wads of gum down the toilet as she may become exposed if they clog the sewer pipes.

There is not a lot to do in Lustville. Men often went to work, raped heavily, or murdered those who stood in their ways, while women often spent their mornings posting selfies on social media, their afternoons spending thousands of dollars on useless trinkets, and their evenings cheating on their partners.

However, there is a rule, another one of those unspoken ones in Lustville. Each and every woman in town must purchase at least six new items every day as a way to prove that they belong in this world.

Otherwise, their chips would begin to beep as a sign of difference, and they would immediately shatter. The women in Lustville generally have no issues when it comes to abiding by this rule. They are in this world for a reason. They were brought here because they no longer wanted to have their own voices and wanted the chance to have what everyone else has.

Many nights, Fourteen dreams about going back home, her real home. She wishes she had known about the nightmare Lustville was capable of becoming before she decided to sneak in. However, she is not allowed to leave this world as long as the Lustville people still exist.

People who enter Lustville are stuck in Lustville. They are forbidden to have any contact with the other world to avoid contaminating the "normies." They craved a mindless world where they are able to do and have all that they want, and they got that world.

There is no turning back.

Unless. Unless Fourteen can find a way to stop the chip and turn everyone in town back to normal. Only then, would the other world allow them to return back to their original lives.

Although Fourteen took part in the research and the creation of the chip, she does not possess all the knowledge of the chip. Her best friend and colleague, Charlotte Densen, is the main creator and the people of Lustville's, and her, only chance of living a normal life again.

However, Charlotte had also been infected by the chip, and she had turned from a prestigious neuroscientist to a ditzy influencer and adulterer.

"Here we go again. Another day of useless, mindless shopping for shit I just chuck inside my closet." Fourteen grunts to herself, as she squeezes her feet into her tight black platform shoes and leaves her apartment to do her daily shopping.

Fourteen is not a materialistic person. Not at all. She hates the idea of using objects in attempts to replace true happiness and self-satisfaction. She has no problem with other people being consumed by materialism, but Fourteen would rather spend her time and money on adventures and travels, experiences that could not be replaced, moments she could cherish forever.

Swinging her $8,000 Prada handbag and throwing on a fake smile, Fourteen joins the rest of the women in Lustville, also swinging handbags and fake smiling, on the streets. They are all dressed in long silver dresses while wearing black platform shoes, and they all say "hello" to people they walk past even though they don't truly mean it.

'This is like a freaking horror movie. Everyone is a damn clone!' Fourteen thinks to herself.

Because she does not technically have the chip inside her brain, any opinionated thoughts she has that contradict popular beliefs would not trigger her demise and cause her to shatter. She only needs to remember to keep her thoughts inside her mind and not expose them to the public. The chip cannot destroy her, but the people sure can.

After saying "hello" to about 150 different people and trying not to break character, Fourteen finds herself standing in front of The Glam, the most obnoxiously decked out building Fourteen has ever seen, with people literally dressed in sterling silver as they walk out of it, and she goes in.

'I want to puke.' Fourteen thinks to herself as she comes face to face with the highly decorated interior of the building, completely filled with wide-eyed soulless creatures greedily destroying each other for the tiniest of rings.

'Alright, let's just get this over with.'

Fourteen steps onto the lush silver velvet rug and finds herself surrounded by dozens upon dozens of chandeliers and candelabras. Every wall and every crevice of the building are adorned with metallic silver and gold embellishments, as the reflections from the glaring sun blind her wherever she turns.

After sixty brutal minutes of aimlessly wandering around and PRETENDING to adore all the items in the store (sixty minutes is the minimum amount of time women in Lustville are allowed to "window shop"), she stops by one seemingly empty counter, calls the salesman over, who looks like he had just stepped out of a hair gel factory, and she randomly picks out the first six jewelry pieces from around the store that she can see, with zero care as to what they look like and trying hard to not fall asleep as the salesman describes, in excruciating detail, that the pieces she had picked out also comes in a variety of stones and colors.

"You look like an amethyst girl. How about I go into the back and get you some gorgeous cuts of amethyst and emerald to go with your dazzling eyes?" The salesman continues.

"Thanks, but I think these pieces would do just fine." Fourteen replies.

"Oh, stop being so humble! You deserve the best! Now, how about you just wait right here, and I'll go fetch them for you!" He insists, as he flies off like a fairy toward the back of the store.

A few minutes later, he dances back with a large tray, covered in a variety of different stones.

"And here we have…"

"I'll take them all!" Fourteen exclaims, interrupting the salesman as she hands over her credit card.

She does not have the patience for him to describe all 73 stones on that tray. She just wants to get the hell out of that bedazzled store. Besides, it's not like she's spending her own money anyway.

"Alrighty, then! Let me just go package these up for the beautiful queen."

Fourteen watches as the salesman prances off to the register.

Out of the corner of her eye, she notices a group of young women lashing insults out at one another, calling each other "slut" and "whore," over one little bracelet. Some women in Lustville like to engage in competitions. In this one, "The Whore-Off" as Fourteen likes to call it, whichever woman can make the rest of the group trigger their sadness emotion first, wins.

Minutes later, the salesman comes prancing back with her credit card and roughly 30 little shopping bags, his silver pressed suit shining brightly beneath the sun roof. Fourteen takes them from his hands, leans in so he can snap a selfie of the two of them together (taking selfies has become the new version of saying "thank you"), and leaves the store, dreading having to repeat this nightmare the next day.

CHAPTER 4

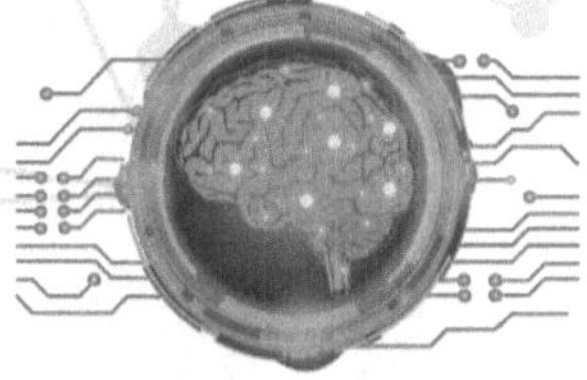

EIGHT ROLLS back onto her side of the bed, completely naked, relaxed, and satisfied. The strapping man beside her gets up almost immediately and walks into her silver-tiled bathroom. Eight admires Nine's magnificent figure from afar.

He is extremely tall and broad-shouldered, with washboard abs that define his body. He has silver white curls that reach up to his ears, dark eyes hidden behind long black lashes, and the most perfect jawline decorated by the slightest hint of a silver white stubble.

As pleasing as he is to the eyes, Nine is even more pleasing in bed. Eight smiles as she reflects on the intense and passionate love they had just shared moments ago. Nine had caressed her and kissed her in all the right places, and had made Eight moan numerous times.

Suddenly feeling shy, Eight wraps the silver satin sheets around her naked body and lies back down, watching the ceiling fan whirl continuously in circles.

It is a cold winter afternoon. Eight looks outside her window, through her silver curtains, and sees the snow beginning to flurry down. The sun shines fiercely down onto her apartment complex, and its heat creeps inside Eight's opened bedroom windows, warming her exposed toes from underneath her silver satin sheets.

Eight hears Nine turn on the shower. She knows that he will leave immediately after, as true feelings of intimacy are not common in Lustville. However, Eight does not mind it much, for intimacy is not something she craves. It is an unfamiliar concept to her, and she cannot remember a time when she truly felt in love.

Suddenly, she hears the front door sling open. Nine is still in the shower so it could not have been him leaving. Unalarmed, Eight stands up from her bed and wraps herself in her long silver robe. She slowly tiptoes up to her bedroom door, which is slightly ajar. Through the slit, she peeks into the living room and sees her husband, Ten, standing at the front door.

"EIGHT!" Her husband yells, his voice heavy and loud.

Hearing the loud voice of Eight's husband, Nine re-enters the bedroom from the adjoining bathroom. He has a towel wrapped around his groin, but other than that, he is stark naked. Even at that critical moment, Eight finds herself admiring the way Nine's curls, now damp, falls back from his head. His wet lashes give definition to his dark and beautiful eyes.

However, only after seconds of admiring Nine, Ten slams open the bedroom door, and the two men come face-to-face, with Ten scowling and frowning while Nine smiling and smirking. Eight looks over at both men, and for the first time ever, she feels a sinking feeling in her stomach.

Eight has never been loyal to Ten. In the past three years of their marriage, she has slept with numerous people, men and women included. However, Ten never minded as fidelity is not a concept known to either of them.

In fact, Ten is not loyal to Eight either. She had come home, many times, finding Ten in bed with several different women, neighbors and friends included.

Did they yearn for loyalty? Perhaps. Eight does find herself occasionally wondering about what it would be like to have a faithful partner and to be faithful to a partner in return.

However, such thoughts were always short-lived. Her mind does not allow her to entertain these preposterous feelings; her head always aches and pains whenever these thoughts come into her mind.

However, Nine is different. For Eight, Nine is just another affair. For Ten, however, it is a different issue. Eight knew what she was getting herself into the moment she ripped off Nine's silver dress shirt. After all, Nine is Ten's biggest business rival.

Nonetheless, she continues to admire Nine, caressing his naked body, biting his lips, and sucking on his rock-solid shaft as Ten stares at the two of them together, emotionless and unmoved. Nine pushes Eight off him, gathers his clothes from the floor, dropping his towel and allowing Eight to lick his shaft several more times in front of Ten, before walking out the door, and home to his wife.

Eight feels the sinking feeling in her stomach expand and seep into her heart, and her headache intensifies in response to it. She slowly makes her way into bed and sits down in attempts to compose herself.

Ten walks over and sits down next to her.

"Eight, I've never cared about your affairs. But, why did you have to choose Nine out of all the men you could have had? You know he is my rival." Ten says, calmly.

"Why should I care about your animosity with Nine?" Eight replies, almost immediately and unconcernedly.

As she speaks, she can feel her head throb even more, as if her brain is swelling and pushing against her skull. Is she starting to feel something toward this situation? Is she starting to care about what she had done? Is she starting to feel guilty? What is guilt anyway?

"It's not about caring, Eight. It's about business. You know he could hurt our income, the income that I support this household and your wardrobe with. Well, anyway, what's happened has happened. Now I have a legitimate reason to get rid of him. Now I can abolish him." Ten states, almost too calmly.

Suddenly feeling nauseated, Eight walks into her closet to change. She cannot brush off this bothersome feeling like there is something wrong. She winces as she feels daggers digging into her brain.

Dropping her bathrobe, she pulls a long silver dress over her head and opens it down over her legs. She walks past her husband, who is eating out another woman on their kitchen countertop, and leaves the apartment.

Eight has no idea where she is going. She just felt the need to leave her apartment. She walks off into the streets and sees that everyone and everything around her are picture perfect, smiling like they had just rolled out of a modeling catalog and addressing those around them like greeting cards, with nothing out of place.

Eight has only ever felt this headache once before, right before she became betrothed to Ten, and had questioned whether she should have stabbed the old man who crashed her wedding.

Little did she know, that old man was her father, but she could not recognize him at the time. However, that headache quickly subsided when she stopped questioning the rules of society and whether her thoughts were justified.

That is until now. Eight finds herself experiencing an even more intense headache than she had experienced in the past. The headache has now succeeded the sinking feeling in her stomach. Eight does not know how to get over this feeling. For the first time in five years, Eight feels conflicted.

Eight continues to walk a few blocks down to a nearby forest to calm her thoughts. She climbs up a hill, sits at the peak, and stares off into town.

After pushing her conflicting thoughts aside, her headache quells and the sinking feeling in her stomach disappears. Feeling like herself once again, Eight heads home.

Walking into her apartment, Eight sees her husband's figure sitting on the silver sofa, crouched over his laptop. Nine and Ten could have been twins; they look physically alike. Like Nine, Ten is also extremely tall and broad-shouldered, with defined muscles. He also has silver white curls, but slightly shorter than Nine's.

Eight looks over at the ticking clock and sees that it is almost midnight. She had forgotten about dinner! Hurriedly, she pulls out a pot from the cabinet and boils some water so she could make their nightly dinner meal of plain white rice and boiled chicken.

Cooking is a woman's only job in her town as Eight is not well-versed in anything else. However, despite this, Eight believes it is a fair trade-off for being able to buy anything and everything she wants with her husband's money without having to get a real job.

Ten is aware of Eight's presence but makes no attempt to talk to her. Eight knows that Ten is not bothered by her; there is no reason for him to be. He is completely apathetic to what had happened between her and Nine. If Eight guessed right, Ten's biggest agenda right now is to murder Nine.

Ten always took great pride in his killings. He is a popular murderer, admired for his skills by those around him. For that reason, everybody attempts to always be on Ten's good side.

Eight had married Ten because they are physically compatible. They are deeply and sexually attracted to each other, and the chemistry between them is out of this world. People in Lustville marry each other solely based on sexual attraction. Eight has yet to meet a man who attracts her as much as Ten attracts her, but if she does, she would have no problem moving on.

There are no ties between Eight and Ten that cannot be broken. Their marriage could easily be shattered with the snap of a finger and neither of them would think anything of it.

However, Eight has no immediate plans to leave Ten. Nine might have been attractive and a great lover, but he still does not match up to Ten's regal.

This thought reminds Eight that she has not yet posted about Nine on her social media platforms. She quickly scrolls through the photos in her phone for the selfie she had taken with Nine while they were in bed and posts it on all her socials with #mynewcatch.

Everybody in town knows of the professional animosity between Nine and Ten. Eight is sure that she would be congratulated for her top-notch affair by all her friends. Nonetheless, somehow this knowledge only leaves her feeling uneasy.

Just like how Ten is a lucrative murderer, Eight is a lucrative adulterer. She engages in long and devastating affairs, primarily with married men. Eight also takes great pride in her status as an adulterer. Many wives struggle to have meaningful and enjoyable extramarital affairs.

Eight has never struggled to do so. She almost always has a partner in addition to Ten, who were almost always great lovers and always physically attractive. However, at that moment, Eight begins to question what she is doing, shaking her head to try and dispel each passing thought.

As soon as she finishes cooking, Eight calls Ten over, who swiftly waltzes into the kitchen. He plops himself down on his usual silver kitchen chair while Eight bustles around setting the plates and utensils. Eight watches as Ten stares at the picture she had posted with Nine on BLykeMe. Without even as much as a wince, he moves onto the next picture.

Suddenly, Eight feels the sinking feeling returning, but she distracts herself with other thoughts to prevent the screeching headache from returning.

The silence between Eight and Ten is deafening.

However, Ten soon breaks the silence.

"I have the perfect plan to murder Nine." Ten claims, calm and composed.

"Oh? What is it?" Eight questions, nonchalantly.

"It's a secret." Ten whispers, driving suspense.

He looks content with whatever plan he has concocted. However, Eight could not care less about how Ten plans to kill Nine. In fact, she does not care at all about Nine's potential death. Is she supposed to care?

Later that night, Eight prepares for a good night's rest, hoping to relax her mind and stop her thoughts from reoccurring. After clearing the dishes, Eight gets ready for bed. To her delight, Ten had gone out for the night, probably to sleep with their neighbor next door. Eight has the entire bed and apartment to herself, falling asleep as soon as her head hits the pillows.

Eight wakes up the next morning to find Ten's side of the bed still empty, albeit slept on.

'He must have slipped into bed and left early, only sleeping for a few hours.' Eight thinks to herself.

Feeling refreshed and more like herself again, Eight gets out of bed and jumps into the shower. As she stands under the shower head, with the sharp lines of water pouring down her body, she plans the rest of the day for herself.

Women in Lustville do not have jobs. They stay home and complete domestic chores. Hence, Eight occupies herself with household work for the rest of the day, leaving her apartment only twice, once to buy herself three diamond rings from The Glam, and once to purchase three new pairs of pumps from a local shoe store called "The Heel."

The rest of the week goes by smoothly. Ten had made no further comments about Nine, and Eight had found her life returning to normal as well. She has also begun flirting with a potential new lover, Eleven, an exhibitionist who fornicates with her whenever they step foot out in public.

However, this peace does last long.

Exactly a week later, Eight wakes up one day to find Ten already gone, as usual. Eight had noticed the laundry hamper piling up yesterday, so she decides that she would devote her time today toward laundry. Little does she know, this is not just another ordinary day.

After a quick shower, Eight dresses herself in a long silver dress. As she stands in front of the mirror brushing her hair, Eight finds a tired-looking woman staring back at her. She has silver white hair that falls down to her waist in cascading waves. She looks quite short and has a womanly figure with lush curves and full breasts.

She looks perfectly healthy, except for the presence of slight dark circles under her eyes and the strange electric shocks protruding from the top of her head.

Unconcerned, Eight brushes it off.

After getting ready, Eight walks into the kitchen to make herself some breakfast. Ten usually leaves very early in the morning so Eight mostly eats breakfast by herself. She fixes herself some rice cakes and half a grapefruit, along with a mug of black coffee, and she gulps it all down in barely ten minutes. She then starts the washing machine to get the laundry going and lazily lies down on the sofa, turning on her favorite soap opera.

Snuggling up underneath her soft silver blanket, Eight hears her phone vibrate just as she turns on the television. It is a BLykeMe notification. Thinking that it is just one of her posts getting a verified comment, Eight opens it to find a photo that her husband had tagged her in. The graphic photo shows Ten kneeling down next to a mutilated body, smiling. The body is backside up, so Eight struggles to identify who it was.

This is not unusual for Eight. Ten has a reputation for being an infamous killer, and people in town often boast about their greatest kills. Eight then reads the caption, which says, "Just killed my rival and my wife's special friend."

The sinking feeling returns to Eight's stomach. After a week of peace and quiet, she feels her head beginning to throb again. What is wrong with her? Why does murder bother her suddenly when it never has before?

Eight stares closer at the photo, recognizing the location. It is the front of her apartment building!

Turning off the television, Eight races downstairs and out the front door, finding a group of people gathered around in a circle. In the middle, stands Ten, smiling over Nine's dead body and holding a large and bloody butcher knife in his right hand. The crowd of people all laugh, cheer, and applaud Ten.

Eight would have done the same, as she usually does, but this time is different. This time, all she feels is the queasy, sinking feeling.

Eight can feel her entire body sway with a sensation that pulsates throughout her entire body. Suddenly, she hears a beeping noise inside her head.

She has heard these beeps before, as has everyone, for they

are not uncommon. Most people have heard beeping noises in their heads at one point in time, and they all fear the reason as to why.

An ambulance pulls up, and the paramedics slowly load Nine's decapitated body onto a stretcher. There is no attempt to resuscitate him or to punish Ten for his murder. Instead, Ten is lauded as the hero of the whole incident.

Is that not how it is supposed to be?

Eight does not know or understand why, but she begins to question the series of events that had just happened and how it seems immoral, regardless of everyone cheering. She finds her headache progressing further and the sinking feeling enhancing.

By now, she experiences that feeling leave her stomach and enter her bloodstream; she can feel it shake her very body to the core. Eight tries hard to calm herself but nothing seems to help. Her head is still quietly beeping.

Giving up, she walks back into her apartment, lies on her sofa, closes her eyes, and slowly drifts off.

Eight wakes up around midnight again with Ten hovering over her body, still bloody. The uneasy feeling had disappeared, and her head is no longer beeping.

"Dinner." He says, smiling like a child in a chocolate factory.

For a minute, Eight thought that Ten had prepared dinner for the both of them. However, she soon realizes he is only demanding for her to make dinner, now that she is awake. She stands up and rushes to the kitchen, fixing her dress and hair along the way. She quickly sets pots and pans on the stove and begins to boil water.

While preparing dinner, Eight tries to not think about what had happened today, lest her headache returns. Nonetheless, she could not stop thinking about it. Why does murder bother her suddenly? What is that sensation, that sensation that overpowers all her senses, and makes her head beep?

Throwing these unanswered questions aside, she sits down for dinner with Ten.

"What happened to you?" Ten asks, uninterestedly.

"Nothing, I just feel a little sick, that's all." Eight replies, meekly.

"Well, maybe you're sick. You should go see a doctor."

"No."

"Okay, as you wish. Anyway, do you want to hear the details of how I killed Nine?"

"No. Can we please just eat dinner?"

Eight begins to feel queasy again.

"Sure. But what's wrong? You've always wanted to hear about my murders. Are you sure you're fine?"

Feeling defeated, Eight asks, "Ten, have you ever felt an overwhelming and trembling sensation in your body that makes your head beep?"

Ten looks back at Eight, his eyes wide and fearful.

"You know that's fatal territory you're treading on, right? You know what happens to those who do not suppress their thoughts, right?" Ten whispers, quietly.

"Yes, Ten. I don't need you to remind me."

Eight truly did not need any reminders of what happens to people who experience beeps in their heads. She used to have a friend, Twelve, who lived in the apartment next to hers. Twelve and Eight often hung out when their husbands were at work and even shared their extramarital partners. At the beginning, Twelve made no complaints about her life; instead, she rather enjoyed it.

However, as time passed by, Twelve began to change.

Twelve started to lose interest in infidelity, believing that it was wrong. She then started to behave erratically, often shedding tears when she found her husband with other women and whenever he killed, stole, or lied. Eight has only ever cried when her eyes were irritated, out of physical necessity.

Twelve soon began to complain to Eight about her head beeping. But, Eight paid no heed to Twelve and always disregarded what she said.

Besides, why should she care?

However, one day, while Twelve and Eight were walking around a nearby forest, Twelve began to scream and cry uncontrollably after seeing one stranger kill another, causing everyone around them to stare, confused and cautious.

Twelve made an appeal to Eight, asking her to stop the murder from happening. However, Eight refused to do so.

Why would she do such an unnecessary and silly thing?

Why should she?

After all, murders are such a normal part of human behavior.

Twelve's entire body began to tremble, and her head began to writhe from the torment of nonstop beeping. Despite knowing the consequences, Twelve ran to the crime scene to try and nab the murderer, but before she could reach him, she plummeted to the ground.

Eight watched, with her jaw wide open, as Twelve shattered into a million pieces right before her eyes. Twelve might have been human, but she shattered into pieces as if she was made of glass. Her broken pieces lay, still, on the grassy forest ground. Only a box-like object remained intact, a dark black box with a fluorescent yellow center.

That was the first time Eight had ever seen something like that happen. She always thought it was a rumor that people who become "mentally unfit" disintegrate into pieces, never believing it until she saw it happen with Twelve.

With Twelve's death, Eight constantly has to remind

herself that the only way to stay alive is to follow the unspoken rules of Lustville without questioning them.

It was the first time that she had realized that her mind and body are connected. Eight's head continues to beep while she reminisces on this.

Eight desperately wants the images and thoughts of Twelve's death out of her mind, so she tries to distract herself by asking Ten about his day. Ten, always eager to talk about business, begins rambling on about stock markets and trade. However, Eight only ever pretends to be interested for her peace of mind, never truly understanding or knowing any part of her husband's life.

Over the next month or so, Eight tries to forget about the memory of Twelve and the murder of Nine. Usually, forgetting a past lover is easy for Eight as she never lets herself become emotionally attached to her lovers. This time though, the image of Nine's dead body continues to haunt Eight's dreams. However, it is not the thought of missing him that affects her. Rather, it is his gruesome death that plagues her mind every night.

Whenever she thinks about his death, her head throbs, and she begins to tremble uncontrollably.

Fed up with her persistent headaches, Eight soon decides that the best remedy from her headaches is to distract her entire being into her new lover, Eleven. Her relationship with Eleven is passionate, intimate, and drives her sexually insane, but he recently got married and is on his honeymoon overseas. Desperate, Eight looks for a new partner until Eleven returns.

Eight does not usually participate in temporary arrangements. Of course, all her affairs were temporary, but they all lasted for at least six months. Most people usually change affairs after about one month, like Ten does.

Eight could have easily waited for Eleven to come back home to pursue intercourse with him, but she needed to distract her mind from her constant thoughts of morality. So, she decides to call up the one man she knows who would be interested, Thirteen.

Thirteen had expressed an interest in Eight many years back, an interest that he had continued to pursue over the years. Eight is aware of Thirteen's love interest toward her, but she never got together with him because there was always someone better. Thirteen is famous for having very short affairs, the complete opposite of Eight. Now that she is bored, she rings him up to see what he has to offer.

Eight sets up a date with Thirteen for lunch that afternoon at a restaurant that she had picked out. Thirteen was already seated and drinking a glass of Merlot when she arrived. The cozy and quaint restaurant is located in the heart of the busy city, and it is one of Eight's favorite restaurants as it is often known for prostitution.

Seeing Eight, Thirteen jumps up and helps her into her seat. Thirteen is handsome, but Eight had never been particularly attracted to him. He is not that tall, just slightly taller than Eight. He is also lanky, with slender limbs. Thirteen has silver white hair, just like Ten, Nine, and all the other men in town.

Thirteen offers to pour Eight some wine. As he does so, Eight notices blood stains on his fingers but decides to let it go and not question him about it.

"I ordered you your favorite dish. I have been following your BLykeMe feed for years so I know everything about you." Thirteen begins the conversation.

"I don't care. I'm going to get straight to the point. I want us to have an affair." Eight replies.

Hearing this, Thirteen's eyes widen and a smile appears on his face.

"That's amazing!! And perfect timing too! I've been looking for a new affair. My wife is starting to bore me. When do we start?" Thirteen asks, eagerly, jumping up and down like an excited puppy.

"Come over to my apartment tomorrow around noon. I'll be waiting for you." Eight answers, seductively.

The next day, Thirteen shows up, right on time. They watch a movie about killer phones while sitting awkwardly on the sofa, but soon end up in bed, having sexual intercourse at least six times, as expected. Thirteen is a surprisingly good lover, and Eight enjoyed it more than she had predicted. Not once did her thoughts about the past and about Nine's murder pop into her head during her time with him.

Thirteen walks out of her apartment a few hours later, leaving both him and Eight satisfied. Assuming that this was just a one-time affair, Eight expected to never see Thirteen again. She was wrong. She receives a text from him within an hour of him leaving, asking her when he could come back for another round. Reluctant and feeling slightly guilty of what she is doing, she pushes aside her piercing headache, once again, and agrees to see him again.

After a week of sleeping and fooling around with Thirteen, Eight's interest in him begins to deteriorate. Their relationship was fun and different at the beginning because Thirteen was new and exciting, but Eight quickly begins to realize how dull he actually is. Even the sex, which was passionate and lustful at first, became more of a chore than an activity.

However, Thirteen refuses to call it quits on Eight. He wants her, and he refuses to stop pursuing her. He shows up at her apartment even when he is not invited, and he calls and texts her every night, telling her how much he misses her. He gives his full attention to her whenever he is with her.

Thirteen is more attentive to her than any of her previous lovers. Still, Eight is not interested and begins to regret ever asking Thirteen to start an affair, now feeling like she is being stalked.

"I want to end our fling." Eight bluntly tells Thirteen.

"No." Thirteen retorts.

"What do you mean 'no'? I want out. I'm tired of you."

"I mean no. I like you a lot. In fact, I think I love you. I refuse to accept that we are over."

"Love? What? No! Please leave me alone."

"Eight, please. Please, let's continue." By this point, Thirteen's voice has become more high-pitched. He gets down on his knees, begging, with tears flowing down his cheeks.

"Please." Thirteen pleads, while still crying.

Before Eight has a chance to speak, Thirteen's head begins to beep. Memories of Twelve's and Nine's death flood Eight's mind with thoughts of morality once again. The sinking feeling in her stomach returns. Her head begins to throb, and she can hear the beeping noise inside her own head.

Pushing aside her instincts, Eight cannot bear to watch Thirteen shatter the same way that Twelve had shattered. She does not know why, but an urge came over her telling her to intervene. She needs to find a way to help Thirteen before he also disintegrates.

She gets up from the sofa and walks into the kitchen. Thirteen does not follow her. He remains in the same position, on his knees, staring at the silver carpet. Eight searches the kitchen cabinets and finds one of Ten's guns, the same gun he used to kill Nine.

Holding it in her sweaty palm, shaking, Eight walks back into the living room, where Thirteen's head is now beeping faster.

Thirteen sees the gun in Eight's hand and begins to panic, unsure of what she will do but pleading her to stop regardless. His head beeps louder with each plead, and his cries make Eight feel even more uneasy. With one eye closed, she points the gun at Thirteen's head and pulls the trigger. Thirteen falls onto the ground, with his eyes and mouth wide open. His blood splatters onto her long silver dress and stains the carpet.

Eight freezes, unable to move.

'What the hell just happened?' She thinks to herself.

She has never killed anyone before. What came over her? After a minute of shock, she drops the gun and places two fingers on his neck. No pulse. He is dead. She had killed Thirteen.

Eight was expecting to feel calm and relief from killing Thirteen and putting him out of his misery. Instead, she feels a different sensation coursing throughout her body. This sensation is not like the usual; it is much heavier, yet strangely better. She closes her eyes and drifts off as she sits back down onto the sofa, startled by her husband's voice moments later.

"Good God! What have you done?" She hears her husband loudly exclaim.

Eight opens her eyes to find Ten standing over Thirteen's dead body, which has nearly been drained of blood. He bends down and feels around Thirteen's body for a pulse. Nothing. He searches Thirteen, pulls out his wallet and phone, and walks into their bedroom. Eight is now truly a murderer.

Still startled and confused, Eight just wants this feeling of guilt to vanish so she could feel indifferent about everyone around her again. Indifference was all she had ever felt toward anyone and anything. Instead, she feels a rush of sensation overtake her body as she cannot stop shivering.

With a huge grin slapped on his face, Ten quickly returns, whips out his phone, and takes a selfie with Thirteen's carcass.

"I'm so proud of you, and I can't wait to tell everyone in town about it. My wife is a killer, just like me." Ten exclaims to Eight, planting a light kiss on her cheek.

Eight tries to bask in the glory like her husband, but struggles to do so. The sensation continues to overwhelm her. The only solution, she thinks, is to murder all her lovers from this point on in order to make herself stronger and less vulnerable when it comes to death. After all, it is only fair to Thirteen if she does.

Right?

CHAPTER 5

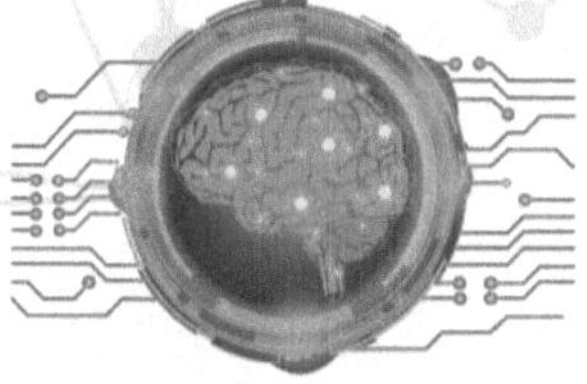

MORE THAN TWO months have passed since Thirteen's death. Eight no longer loses sleep over him because Eleven is scheduled to return from his honeymoon soon.

Eleven is amazing in every aspect and completely compatible with Eight. Not to mention the fact that Eleven is physically a sight to behold as well. His muscles and abs peek from underneath his silver dress shirt, and Eight always finds herself staring at them.

When they make love, Eight likes to trace his well-defined body with her finger. Eleven has a rugged face and clean-cut and styled silver white hair. He also has the most attractive set of eyes, which shines brighter than the sky beneath the sun.

Their relationship was going well, until it all changed.

One afternoon, Eleven stops by Eight's apartment after work, as usual, to have intercourse with her. However, instead of the pleasurable sensations she is used to experiencing with Eleven, Eight feels a dull, but sharp, pain running through her pelvis and around her hips, which continues to persist even after Eleven leaves.

In attempts to ignore it, Eight grabs a heating pad, places it on her lower abdomen, and switches on the television to watch a fiction movie about a world where everyone is free to have their own individual thoughts. She takes some painkillers and about an hour into the film, she dozes off.

She wakes up to the sound of Ten showering. Eight gets up, hoping the pain had subsided while she was asleep, but the discomfort is still there. She prepares dinner for herself and her husband, and he demands that she has intercourse with him to relieve his stressful day.

Because of an unspoken rule, Eight is not allowed to say no, or both her and Ten will shatter. As he moves in and out of her, the pain worsens, and she begins to bleed, not with blood, but with a black and viscous liquid substance that oozes out of her.

Panicking, she runs to the nearest hospital. By the time she gets there, the pain has become so intense that she falls over and collapses.

Days later, Eight wakes up on a hospital bed, confused as to how she got there. Her doctor explains to her that she has STX, a form of STI that causes her pelvis to devour into itself and liquefy. Eight is shocked.

An STX? Even though STXs are quite common in their society, Eight begins to question how she got one, realizing that one, or multiple, of her partners must have lied about their history. Because almost everyone in town has been infected by STXs, hospitals no longer offer treatment or antibiotics as people have stopped caring.

Eight goes home and finds Ten lying on the sofa, mindlessly clicking through channels. She walks up to him, nervously, and tells him that she has an STX.

However, to her surprise, Ten shrugs it off and continues to stare at the television. Taken aback by his indifference, Eight drops the subject and goes to bed, afraid of starting a fight if she continues to pursue.

The next morning, Eight texts Eleven and asks him to come over. Expecting more sex, Eleven eagerly skips over to her apartment, only to find a stern and angry woman standing at the door.

"Eleven, I have an STX. Why didn't you tell me you're infected?" Eight asks as soon as he steps into her apartment.

"Eight, I don't have an STX. That's disgusting. Why would I tell you about something I don't have? I couldn't have passed it onto you." Eleven replies, looking genuinely confused and irritated that they are arguing instead of having sex.

Seeing the questioning look on Eleven's face, Eight wonders for a moment whether Eleven is telling the truth. However, there is no one else who could have passed it onto her so she continues to press for answers.

"STOP LYING! IT IS YOU!" Eight shouts at Eleven, blowing him back in the process.

"NO, IT'S NOT! STOP ACCUSING ME, YOU FILTHY WHORE!" Eleven shouts back.

Anger and pain flushes through them as both their heads throb. Eight sits down on the sofa to recollect her sanity. So does Eleven.

After several moments of silence, Eight speaks up.

"I'm going to pause our affair until I can figure this out." Eight whispers.

"Fine with me." Eleven sternly replies, as he stands up and silently walks out of her apartment.

Eight continues to sit on the sofa, pondering over Eleven's denial. He didn't seem like he was lying, but people in Lustville are also notorious liars. However, his look of confusion was so genuine that Eight feels herself doubting whether it truly was Eleven who gave her the STX.

Who else could it have been though?

Two days later, Eight receives a text from Eleven, telling her that he is also experiencing symptoms of a STX. He proceeds to imply that it was Eight who passed it onto him, which only stabilized it in Eight's mind that it must have been Eleven who gave it to her, and he's just blaming her for it.

He must have contracted it from his wife or someone else he had recently slept with. Men are always lying to get what they want.

Eight knows that Eleven will not leave her because she has the disease. After all, he has the disease too, and thus, it would be hypocritical of him to leave her for it. She is relieved at the thought of not losing her affair. After Thirteen, Eight is not in the right mood or mindset for another short-lived fling.

Later that night, Eight and Ten begin fooling around when Ten suddenly winces in pain, the same pain that Eight had experienced earlier, and black ooze begins leaking out of him.

Wait a minute. Ten was completely indifferent when Eight first told him about her STX, and now he is liquefying in their bed? Could he have been the one who gave it to her?

"Ten, do you have an STX?" Eight questions him while he is still inside of her.

"What? Of course not." Ten replies, moaning as he answers.

Eight scans Ten's face for the truth as his words no longer mean anything to her. His eyes dart back and forth, and his forehead begins to sweat.

"You're lying." Eight retorts, as she realizes what's happening.

Sighing, Ten finishes inside of her, rolls over onto his side of the bed, and confesses.

"Fine, yes, I have an STX. I am the one who gave it to you. I contracted it when I fooled around with some prostitutes during my business trip last summer."

"What!? Why didn't you tell me?!?" Eight shrieks, sitting up on her side of the bed, unconcerned that her head is beginning to beep again.

"Eh, whatever, it's not a big deal. Now, goodnight." Ten says, ignoring her and quickly falling asleep.

Still baffled, Eight continues to shuffle through her conflicting thoughts. How could he do this to her? How could he not though? Why should he care? Everyone has an STX anyway, so why should it be a big deal?

She can feel her eyes flickering back and forth as she ponders, sparks flying out through her head, and her entire body shaking as though electricity is running through her.

The next morning, Eight hears her doorbell ring as she washes the dishes. She was not expecting company and assumes it's the new neighbors who just moved into her building. To her surprise, she sees Eleven standing there as she opens the door.

"I came here to officially end our affair. I can't deal with all this culpability, and the fact that you gave me an STX and then blamed me for it. I'm done." Eleven speaks, abruptly, as soon as he sees her.

Eight's jaw drops. She is shocked. She never expected an STX to ruin her lust life. She wants to continue seeing Eleven, but she knows better than to disagree with the desires of a man.

"Alright. I understand. But before we officially break it off, can we meet up one last time tomorrow afternoon? Not at my apartment, of course, but at some place else. I'll text you the location."

Eleven nods and leaves.

Eight immediately texts Eleven the location of her favorite restaurant. Eleven telling her that their affair is over triggers beeping inside her head, forcing her to have to resort to her master plan of regaining her strength back.

The next morning, Eight wakes up early to properly reflect on her plan. She moves over to the sofa to avoid waking up her husband, who is sound asleep next to her. She has never committed something like what she is planning before, so she must make sure she has all the details locked and verified.

Ten is slightly surprised when he sees Eight's side of the bed empty after waking up an hour later. He finds Eight on the sofa, but he doesn't say anything to her or question her. He assumes that Eight is still upset about the STX. Not wanting to stir up an argument, he takes a quick shower, puts on his silver dress shirt, and bolts out the front door.

That afternoon, Eight prepares for her meeting with Eleven. She psyches herself up by meditating for two hours and listening to calming music. Is she mentally ready for what she is about to do? Probably not. However, she has no other choice.

She opens her closet door, walks into her wardrobe of dozens upon dozens of long silver dresses. She puts one on, tearing a suggestive slit along one side. She then puts on her finest pair of black pumps and curls her silver white hair into flowing locks. She goes into the kitchen, retrieves Ten's small silver gun from one of the cabinets, and slides it under her garter belt before leaving her apartment.

Eleven is already seated by the time Eight arrives. Seeing Eleven begins to make Eight feel queasy, but she brushes off her thoughts and confidently strides towards him. She then takes the gun out from under her dress and points it at Eleven, whose eyes flare open and jaw drops.

Everyone inside the restaurant stops eating and scrambles to take out their phones so they could post the event on BLykeMe.

Eleven remains glued to his chair, paralyzed. Maybe this is the first time that anybody has ever threatened to kill him. After all, he is relatively young, much younger than Eight.

Eight has never killed anybody in public before. She has only ever killed one person, Thirteen, but that was in the privacy of her own home. She could have easily chosen to kill Eleven privately too, but she needed the publicity. She believes the publicity would make her feel better, stronger, and more invincible.

The past few months had really disconnected her from society, especially with Nine's murder and her recurring thoughts of Twelve. She wants to return to her usual self, back to her reality, back to the flawless and nonchalant author and influencer she is known to be.

Eleven stands up from his seat, so Eight redirects her gun toward him. Before Eleven could move or make a run for his life, Eight shoots Eleven straight onto his forehead, causing him to crumble to the ground the same way that Thirteen did. Blood pours onto the bare restaurant tiles, completely bathing them in crimson red.

More people gather at the scene, coming from afar after having heard the shot. They all cheer and applaud Eight.

After shooting Eleven, Eight feels the same sensation that she had felt when she shot Thirteen rush through her body. The sensation warms her skin and sends shivers through her bones. This time around though, Eight refuses to fall victim to her guilt. She must stand strong.

Perhaps just having that attitude works, as Eight feels the sensation slowly subside. Her head did not ache once. To further cement her place back in society, Eight kneels beside Eleven. She searches for a pulse, but finds none, as expected.

Then, with a shaky hand, she takes out her phone from the small clutch she had carried with her.

She opens the camera and forces herself to smile as she poses next to Eleven's dead body, and she snaps a picture. The crowd continues to cheer, making Eight feel that much stronger.

She posts the photo onto her BLykeMe account and, for the first time in a long time, Eight feels like her old self again, perhaps even better. Maybe she should write a book about her new skill in murdering scorned lovers.

CHAPTER 6

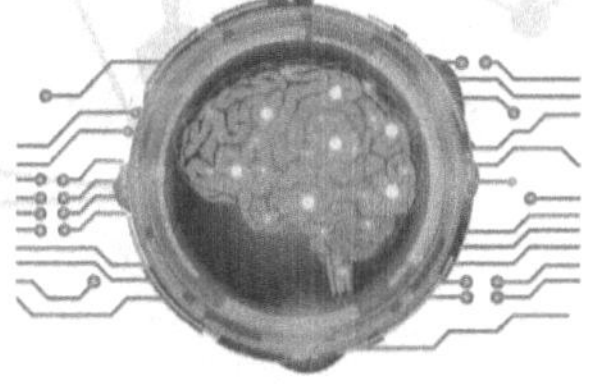

TEN HAS ALWAYS BEEN interested in business, as far as he can remember. Then again, he cannot remember that far back. Ten's earliest recollection of his life is at the age of thirty, just five years back. He cannot remember anything before that time. This used to bother him.

He used to search for answers and clues as to why this is the case until he was warned of the dire consequences he would face if he continued to do so. He had also asked Eight if she could remember her childhood. She could not either, as her earliest recollection is at the age of twenty-five, just five years back also.

In fact, Ten soon discovers that everybody around him only remembers the past five years of their lives.

Five years ago, everyone in Lustville had microchips injected into their brain as part of a psychological experiment, causing them to speak and behave just like everyone around them.

People were no longer able to remember their pasts, their names, or the lives they had before that moment. Because of the chip, if anyone tried to rebel against the commonality of everyone else, the main unspoken rule of the chip, the chip would activate and the person would immediately shatter.

Ten had always worked a normal nine-to-five job as a marketing agent at a small consulting company. People in Lustville were assigned to random jobs when the chips were injected into them. Despite their lives before and the skills they possess, everyone had to completely change their lives and careers.

Men were forced to work menial day-to-day business jobs while women had to become homemakers.

However, men are also given the choice to become entrepreneurs, a given right only men have, if they can make it, that is. A chance to do so came flying at Ten when he married Eight, and for that reason, he likes to call his little enterprise his "wedding gift."

Ten had tried to advertise his idea of a gastronomy food business, where the main source of protein for the meals is the people of Lustville that he murders, to potential investors before, but he was always turned down, forcing him to give up on trying to get funding.

However, the opportunity came up again on the night of his wedding, when he forced his wife to sleep with a potential investor, a rich old man she found repulsive at every sight.

Eight had been aware of Ten's dream of opening his own

food chain. However, she didn't have the affair for him. After marrying Ten, Eight realized that marriage didn't mean that she could not continue to sleep around. She only had sex with Ten's investor to ease him into the idea of her having multiple other affairs.

Ten is smart and savvy, so his business grew rapidly over the next three years. However, neither Eight nor Ten expected it to grow as much as it did, and they basked in the wealth that it brought in.

Ten was projected to make his first million by the end of the third year, when the market hit a sudden depression, and the prospect of making his million quickly faded away. However, he was still determined to make it work despite what it took. Who does honest business anyway?

That is how Ten found himself in a meeting with a top tier government official one Tuesday afternoon. It is a rainy day, and Ten could see raindrops hit the large glass window the governor has in his comfortable cabin. Since it is winter, the days are now much shorter. The grey atmosphere outside greatly dims the room inside, which is lit by a single red bulb.

The whole room is mahogany, with wood paneling on the walls and the floor, and wooden furniture encase the entire room. The governor sits behind a large wooden desk, on a black office chair.

The governor is old, far older than Ten. He is pale, and his patchy skin is so thin that Ten can see his chip. The fluorescent yellow center of the chip glistens from beneath his forehead. Despite the cold, perspiration beads shimmer onto the governor's forehead, which he wipes away with a silver handkerchief.

The governor has sunken eyes, a thin mouth, and smells extremely unpleasant. He is dressed in a silver dress shirt and silver tailored pants, just like everybody else, but his garments look more ancient, old, and rusty. No politician ever looks pleasant anyway. The man sits behind a name tag that spells his name, "Zero," while fiddling with his tie.

"So, Ten, I understand that you want me to invest in your business and pull some strings to throw out your competitors?" The governor, Zero, says, in a loud and demeaning voice.

"Yes." Ten replies, frigidly, from his seat in front of Zero.

Zero inspects Ten from head-to-toe, his ugly eyes scanning the length of Ten's body. He wears a look of apathy, which is mainly the only expression that officials are allowed to have.

"Well, Ten, I don't do charity. I would need something from you too."

"What would that be?"

"You see, Ten, I run a successful human trafficking and prostitution business. I don't know if you're aware of that fact or not."

Ten is, but says nothing.

"Luckily for you, I'm letting you help me with this. You see, business has been slow lately. Kidnapping young women is much more difficult now. You know we don't traffic married women. Too much risk for bloodshed, the husbands would pounce on us. Most women are married now, so it has been difficult finding new replacements. If you can get me at least one new woman for my business who is suitable, I will help you with your business." Zero continues.

Ten is not concerned at all about completing this task. Expanding his business is his top priority, so kidnapping a woman so he could have that is not a big issue for him. Plus, he already has someone in mind.

"You have my word. You'll have her soon." Ten replies, standing up.

He gives Zero a firm handshake and exits the cabin with confident steps.

CHAPTER 7

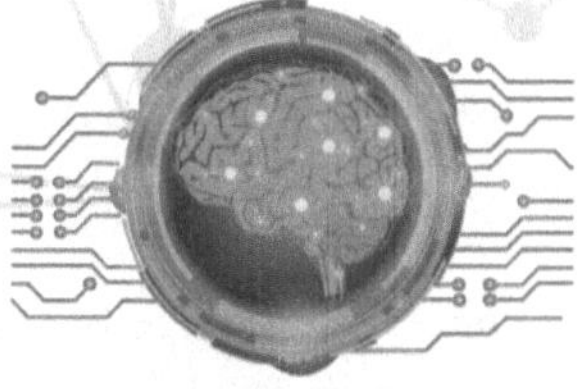

BACK AT HIS APARTMENT, Ten begins plotting a fool proof plan to kidnap his victim, Fourteen. Ten knows where Fourteen lives, for he had meticulously stalked her for weeks before deciding to murder her husband, Nine, so Ten could marry Fourteen. With his deal with Zero, Ten now has a better plan for her.

Ten had kidnapped Nine one morning while he was still asleep. He had bribed the landlord for a copy of the key to Nine and Fourteen's apartment, and he walked in as soon as he saw Fourteen leave. Ten had created a fake alias to lure

Fourteen out of the apartment by pretending to her long-lost sister asking her for help, knowing that she would take the bait as Fourteen always goes out of her way to help others.

Ten drugged Nine, stuffed him inside a sleeping bag, and dragged him to his office. Ten was not willing to sacrifice his precious work hours just for a kill. During lunch, Ten tried to drag Nine back to his apartment so he could kill him. However, Nine woke up suddenly, forcing Ten to kill him on the sidewalk in front of his apartment building instead.

Luckily for Ten, Fourteen would be much easier to lure and capture. She is small and slender, and Ten is confident that he would be able to kidnap her without a threat of challenge. However, despite her size, Fourteen knows that Ten had killed her husband; so, naturally, Fourteen is always cautious when she is around Ten.

Still, how could Ten make sure that Fourteen is the right fit for Zero? What if he spends all this time kidnapping her, and Zero decides to retract his offer to help him? All these thoughts of "what ifs" run through Ten's head, confusing him.

Unable to think clearly, Ten leaves his apartment to go to the local club called "Single Mingles." His last fling had dumped him, so Ten needs another lover to satisfy his desire for infidelity.

While gulping down his fourth shot of Tequila, Ten looks over and sees a young woman sitting down next to him, running her fingers up and down his thighs.

Wanting to grab her by the waist and have his way with her in the bathroom stall, he decides against it so he could save his energy for abducting Fourteen.

Suddenly, a short man comes up to the woman and starts talking to her. Ten gazes at them but remains unaware of what is going on. After five minutes of small talk, the man turns to the bartender for a drink, and the woman walks away. The man then pulls out a packet of mysterious white substance and pours it into the woman's drink, peaking Ten's interest.

She returns, and the man acts nonchalant as if nothing had happened. The bartender also saw what he did but doesn't bother to warn her. Neither does Ten. It was not their place to do so; otherwise, they would be stepping over boundaries, and that is not allowed.

Ten watches as the woman downs her drink and begins to get tipsy almost instantly. Her eyes begin to close, and her body begins to sway back and forth. A few minutes later, the man offers to take the woman home safely and instead, rapes her on top of the pool table and proceeds to lead her out the door.

Raping women is not a sin or a rare occurrence in Lustville. That was not what caught Ten's attention. It was the man's white powder that caught his attention.

Ten has heard about the PCX drug before, but he has never used it or seen it in action. However, now he just might, on Fourteen.

Ten follows the man and woman, hoping to learn more about how to obtain PCX. The man leads the woman into a small room at a shady motel behind the club, completely unaware that he is being followed by Ten.

He locks the door behind him while Ten waits outside, listening to the woman scream in pain, and the man scream in pleasure. An hour later, the man opens the door and finds Ten sitting on the curb.

The man takes one look at Ten, grunts, and proceeds to walk past him.

"Hey, man! Where can I get some of that PCX?" Ten catches the man.

A look of confusion washes over the man's face as he turns around, and then breaks out into a laugh.

"Hold on! Hold on! You mean, you never drugged a woman before?" The man asks, still laughing.

"No, unlike you, I don't need to drug women to get them to go home with me." Ten replies, sarcastically.

"Oh no you didn't just diss me like that! Here, just take this and get out of my sight. I'm sick of you."

Pissed off, the man tosses the small white packet of PCX at Ten and storms off, leaving his one-night stand stranded and unconscious in the room behind him.

Out of lust, Ten walks into the room, where he sees the woman lying on a dirty mattress. Her silver dress is pulled over her head, and her underwear has been thrown onto the floor. After pleasuring himself with the unconscious body, Ten leaves the room and heads home.

The next morning, Ten finds himself in Fourteen's kitchen, spiking her morning pumpkin spice latte with PCX. Fourteen always starts her day off with a pumpkin spice latte, so this would be the perfect trap. Ten hears her walking toward her kitchen so he wedges himself behind her fridge to hide.

Unbeknownst to what Ten had done, Fourteen takes a sip of her latte and immediately collapses onto the kitchen floor. Ten emerges from behind the fridge with thick leather ropes and duct tape, and he ties up Fourteen, throwing her into the trunk of his car while everyone around videotapes them for their live BLykeMe feed.

Almost an hour later, Ten pulls his car up to Zero's cabin and calls him to let him know that he has found Zero's new prostitute. Fourteen is still tipsy and delusional from the PCX, but she has regained enough conscience to the point where she is able to walk.

Fourteen has no idea what she is doing or where she is going, and all Ten could focus on is finally getting his business up and running again.

Ten hustles Fourteen toward the front door, grinning. There is no doorbell, so Ten knocks loudly on the door. After a short wait, a beautiful woman, dressed in full silver lingerie, opens the door and asks Ten what he wants.

"Zero." Ten replies.

The woman's face curves into a seductive smile as she says, "Come in, he's been waiting."

The woman leads Ten and Fourteen up the winding staircase and into the first room on their right. The room is large and expensively decorated. The crimson red and velvet curtains are drawn open, basking the room with bright sunlight. Ten immediately spots Zero lounging, half-naked, on a bed covered with red satin sheets. The woman exits as Zero gets up.

"Well, hello Ten. It's been a while. I thought you had bailed on our plans." Zero says, as he stands up and walks toward Ten.

He pushes Ten aside so he could take a good look at the woman standing behind him. Fourteen sways to and fro, still tipsy, unaware of Zero's presence.

"And I suppose this is the promised young lady? She is a pretty thing. You've done a good job, Ten." Zero applauds.

Zero reaches out a hand toward Fourteen and runs his fingers down her bosom. Fourteen does not flinch at all.

Ten remains silent and still.

"What's her name?" Zero asks.

"Fourteen." Ten replies.

"Well, Ten. You may leave now. I'll get back to you on our deal. First, I need to test her out." Zero says, as he yanks Fourteen's arm and leads her onto his bed.

Ten turns around and walks out the door, confident that Zero would have no issue taking what he wants from Fourteen, as she is still half unconscious.

CHAPTER 8

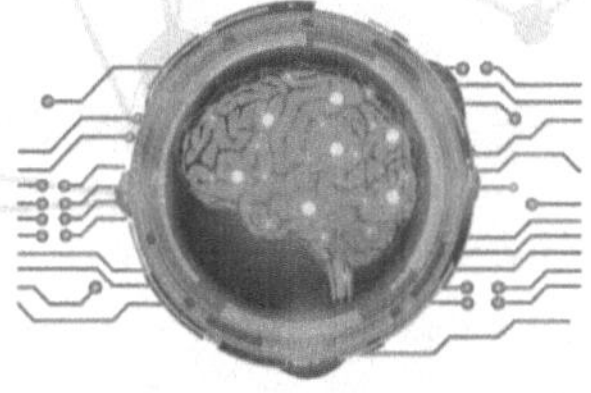

FOURTEEN WAKES UP with a massive headache. She finds herself lying, naked, on cold hard marble rather than on her bed and begins to wonder what had happened. She sits up, trying to recollect her thoughts and memories.

Where is she? Fourteen sees her long silver dress hanging on a sad wooden chair, and her memory begins to return. Before she blacked out from drinking her latte yesterday morning, she saw a strange, but familiar, face peeking out at her behind her fridge. Whoever that was must have drugged her.

Fourteen feels lost, exasperated, and frustrated. She is in an unusual place with no idea how she got there. She looks around and observes her surroundings. She sees hundreds of framed photographs featuring naked women, all with blank stares on their faces.

Suddenly, the door flings open. In walks an old man, with heartless eyes and a round belly. Fourteen recognizes who this man is at first glance. This man is Zero.

Fourteen is familiar with Governor Zero and his popular escort business. He traffics young unmarried or widowed women and prostitutes them off to interested men. Nine had always admired the man's business savvy, but Fourteen thinks it's inhumane and disgusting. Of course, nobody ever cares about her opinions. Everyone around her is heartless and cold.

Suddenly, Fourteen begins to register what is happening. She had been trafficked and sold off into Zero's business. Had Zero already violated her? She sniffs, and she can smell his scent on and inside her. Terrified, she backs away from Zero as he reaches his musty old hands toward her.

"Well, someone looks more awake, now doesn't she?" Zero creepily speaks.

Fourteen refuses to answer. Her mind races back and forth, trying to figure out how to escape.

"You're just perfect. I'm so glad Ten brought you to me. I suspect that you will be my top prize and bring my business back to life." Zero grins widely, flashing his rotting teeth at Fourteen.

'Ten?' Fourteen thinks to herself. 'He kills Nine and then sells me off to this creep? What the hell is wrong with that asshole?!'

Zero inches closer toward Fourteen, forcefully gliding his hand down Fourteen's arm. Extremely uncomfortable, Fourteen grabs Zero's arm and throws it away from her. Zero is taken aback, confused, as women are not allowed to deny the desires of men, but proceeds to put his hand on her again.

Then Fourteen remembers. After Nine's death, she started carrying a pocketknife around in her dress to protect herself from potential killers like Ten. How could she have forgotten that? She begins to slowly inch toward her dress, praying that Zero does not notice.

With her heart beating rapidly against her chest, Fourteen concocts a quick plan inside her head to escape Zero. She could smell the stench of alcohol on him, making her want to throw up. She lets Zero caress her arm, hoping it would distract him long enough for her to grab her knife.

Fourteen cringes at the touch of Zero's rough fingers against her bare skin. She had only ever been touched by Nine in Lustville, forgiving Nine while he had his affairs because she knew the chip inside his head caused him to commit acts of sin. She feels nauseous for letting another man, especially an old and bigot one, grope her.

Inching closer toward her dress as Zero continues to stroke her, Fourteen slowly pulls her knife out from her dress without Zero detecting.

She plunges it into Zero's chest, with strength that she didn't even know she has. Struck by the intense pain, Zero falls back, his blood splattering at Fourteen in the process.

Realizing that she had just stabbed someone, guilt begins to overwhelm her as she sprints down the stairs and out the door, still completely naked. She feels relief once outside, able to breathe again, but still panicking at what had just happened.

After several minutes of running, she stops, looks back, and sees Zero's cabin in the far horizon.

Fourteen has no idea where she is. She has no car and no way of getting home. She still could not believe what Ten did to her. Selling her off like that!? How dare he!?

'Ten.' Fourteen thinks to herself. 'What a fraud. How is he married to such a great person like Eight?'

"Eight!!!" Fourteen screams as she suddenly realizes that Eight might be in danger because she's married to a murderer.

Eight was Fourteen's best friend before the whole "apocalypse," as Fourteen likes to call it. They were co-workers, often working on the same projects and cases in a world-renowned scientific laboratory, specializing in neuropsychology and researching how the human mind responds to the depths of modern society.

In fact, everyone in Lustville had actual names before the apocalypse began, only being assigned a number as they enter Lustville. Fourteen's name was Eve while Eight's name was Charlotte. Eve loved Charlotte like her own sister, and Charlotte loved her just the same. At least, until she was taken away by her own invention.

Eve had managed to escape the apocalypse, unharmed, while most others around her weren't so lucky. They no longer remember their pasts, who they were, or even their names, being assigned numbers in place of them to remove the concept of originality.

They had become robots, clones of one another. Eve watched as her loved ones all lost their personalities and memories, one by one.

Eve had to pretend that she was the same as everyone else in order to survive in the new world of Lustville. People in Lustville have no concept of right or wrong, and they have no doubts when it comes to murdering and manipulating others whenever they feel like it.

Eve had to go against her own instincts and join the crowds in cheering and applauding as she witnessed the murder of person after person, feeling helpless and unable to do anything about it. If she didn't join the popular crowd and her chip didn't beep (because she doesn't have one), she would have surely been killed.

Nonetheless, she has to find a way to rescue Charlotte, to bring her back to her senses because she believes Charlotte is the only one who can end the apocalypse.

But how? Like others, Charlotte is also under the control of the chip in her brain. If Eve attempts to remove the chip to stop the brainwashing, Charlotte would shatter into a million pieces. Eve could not bear to even imagine the thought. She would rather Charlotte live as a clone than not live at all.

The sun had risen by the time Eve makes it back into the city, the next morning. The sun is hidden behind heavy rain-clouds that fill the sky. The temperature dips low, and the cold breeze touches and kisses Eve from behind.

Freezing because she ran out of the cabin completely naked, Eve dresses herself in disease-filled garments she finds in the woods.

Eve fiddles in her tangled locks for a piece of paper, on which she had written down Charlotte's address years ago and had hidden it in her hair. She glances down at it, barely making sense of what she had written, and begins to walk through the cold and dense forest toward Lustville.

CHAPTER 9

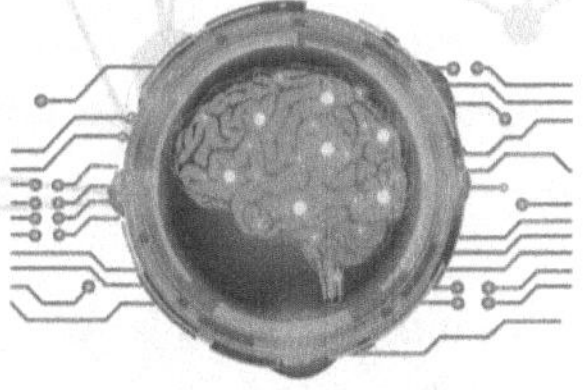

WAKING up on a cold winter morning, Eight draws open her bedroom curtains to observe the weather. The sky looks grey, laden with heavy rainclouds. There is no sign of the sun, and the temperature drops to below freezing. Eight predicts that the cold will freeze her pipelines so she hurries off to take a shower.

After a quick shower, Eight makes herself a daily breakfast of rice cakes, black coffee, and grapefruit. As a social media influencer, her every step is constantly being watched, and she is not allowed to eat anything else besides what she has been told or else she would shatter. She sits at the kitchen table, slowly eating her breakfast when the doorbell rings.

"That's strange, who could that be?" Eight says to herself.

Confused and curious, Eight sips her coffee and stands up to open the door, to her surprise.

In front of her stands a woman. A small woman with silver white hair and tangled locks, wearing a torn up and very dirty long silver dress. She smells like she hasn't showered in years, and her pale skin is stained with dried-up blood.

She stands at the door, fidgeting with her hangnail, as she suddenly looks up and sees a woman with the most perfect face and a sharp jawline. She has big doll eyes, with a small scar running down her left cheek.

Upon seeing Eight, the woman's eyes light up in a way that Eight has never seen from anyone before. Her mouth curves into a smile, and her pupils dance. In the woman's expression, Eight observes liveliness and vivacity that she has never seen in anyone else. It is almost as if the woman seems more…human?

Eight has never seen this woman before, but there is something about her face that triggers a recognition in Eight's mind. Eight feels an invisible force surge through her brain and overpower her whole being in a split second.

She cannot understand or identify what's going on, but she feels an unusual sensation creep down from her brain and into the rest of her body, all the way to her fingers and all the way down to her toes.

It is unlike anything she had ever felt before. Sure, Eight frequently feels the power and surge of passion when she is in bed with one of her partners. While that passion felt amazing, it was still much lighter than what Eight is feeling right now. Passion is only skin-deep; this new sensation encompasses her entire being. Before Eight can recognize what is happening to her body, she hears herself say.

"Eve?"

'Eve? Eight thinks to herself as her chip begins to beep. 'Who the hell is Eve?'

"Yes, Charlotte! It's me, Eve." The woman says, cheerfully. "I don't know how you can remember me since you have that chip attached to your brain, but yes, it's me, Charlotte, your friend, Eve."

The woman's eyes warm into a large smile, and she hugs Eight. Eight stands there, at a loss for words and what to do. Who the hell is Charlotte? What is going on? Nobody has ever hugged her like this before. Nobody has ever hugged her at all. She isn't even sure if hugging is allowed in Lustville.

"I don't remember you. I don't know who you are. I don't even know how I know your name, if that's really your name at all." Eight answers, quietly, and motions for Eve to step inside the house.

However, Eve makes no attempt to go inside. Instead, she continues to stand at Eight's front door. Eve has no interest in seeing the inside of Eight and Ten's apartment. She is afraid of what she might find in there since Ten is an infamous murderer.

"Well, Charlotte, you might not remember me, but I was your friend. Your best friend. Your co-worker. Back before this town became a psychological experiment. Back before these chips that you created took over your brains." The woman continues.

Eight still has no idea what this woman is rambling about as her chip continues to sound. What psychological experiment? When was she ever her friend? She doesn't have friends. She never had a job. What co-worker?

Eight cannot remember beyond the last five years of her life. Is this woman lying? Why would she be? How did they know each other? And most importantly, how could she have created these chips when she doesn't even fully understand the power and function of them?

These questions all race through Eight's mind, clouding her sanity. She is still naïve as to who Eve is and what she is talking about.

However, it feels as if her body understands. Her body responds to Eve by making Eight feel strange, but familiar, sensations. Her head continues to beep, albeit quietly and infrequently.

Suddenly, Eve grabs onto Eight's hand. That ensuing moment feels scarily magical. Eight feels an electric shock run through her arm and cloud her mind. Her vision blurs and causes Eight to see a moving picture through her glassy eyes.

In this picture, Eight is sitting inside a laboratory, leaning over a benchtop with Eve. They are both wearing white lab coats with goggles, and are perusing through articles and textbooks while laughing with each other.

"I don't know what you're talking about. What do you want?" Eight says, terrified, as she snaps back into the present and pulls her arm away from Eve.

"You're right. You probably have no idea what I'm talking about, and there's no way to make you remember either. But let me at least try!"

"How?"

"My dear Charlotte, listen to me carefully because I don't have a lot of time. You see, a couple of years ago, you created a chip, a powerful microchip that singlehandedly controlled the minds of the human population. You used to be a psychology professor and an accomplished scientist. You were successful and won many awards for your work on the human mind.

I'm going to give you the condensed version of what happened, and maybe later, I'll fill you in on the details. A decade ago, everyone in Lustville used to be different, with different personalities, statuses, thoughts, and opinions. Everyone had their own voices and their own minds, and they were able to speak and feel as they pleased. However, relentless competition filled the air and war constantly broke out.

People became jealous of each other and wanted to be just like those around them rather than being themselves. This constant obsession with wanting to be the same as everyone else made them suicidal, and they started killing themselves for not being good enough. You observed the human psyche and decided that the emotionally vulnerable could be healed by a device.

So, you created the device, one that would completely take away the feelings and memories of the emotionally vulnerable. It would wipe out their personalities and grant them their wishes of becoming just like everyone else, where no competition or war would ever occur again.

However, the chip only implanted in the brains of those who were emotionally vulnerable, those who secretly craved acceptance and expressed envy for what they did not have, including you, Charlotte. It tried attaching to my brain, but it fell off shortly after.

Well, pretty soon, the chip created this sub-population of people, this society of clones, who lack feelings, morals, and values because everyone is now the same. Your chip took away the uniqueness and personalities that people naturally have in an attempt to save the world.

Because of this, the rest of the world had to create a new planet for people with chips in them, to ensure that everyone would be exactly the same so hate would never occur again, so everyone could feel like they belong in a perfect society, a society where everyone is free to do what they want without consequences, a society where people could murder and cheat, but still have others praise them, a world where everyone can belong.

Unfortunately, the chip did not function as expected, and if anyone decides to have their own thoughts and opinions, if anyone decides to rebel against the commonality of others and tries to have their own morals and voice, the chip would cause that person to shatter into a million pieces.

You created a world where no one is allowed to be different. I don't belong in this world. I live back home, back where we belong, back on Earth. I only pretended like I am part of this world for my husband and for you." Eve faintly lies in attempts to get Eight to believe her, as she grasps Eight's head between her palms.

Usually, Eight would not be bothered by such slander, but part of her body senses a certain truth in Eve, a certain truth that causes her eyes to suddenly shed tears.

Confusion and disbelief overwhelm Eight. What Eve said cannot not be true. Eight could not have been a scientist. Women are not allowed to work. Eve is probably delusional.

"I don't believe you. You're lying. You're crazy! I don't know you. I'm not a scientist or a professor. I didn't create this stupid chip!" Eight retorts in disbelief.

"I understand it's hard, but please believe me, Charlotte. I am telling you the truth. You need to believe. Your husband tried to prostitute me off to Governor Zero AND he killed my husband, and everyone here is STILL applauding him. That's not normal in the world you used to live in! His type of behavior would normally have gotten him thrown into prison for life in the world you came from, the world of social order and morality. This world allows people to commit acts of sin that were not tolerated back on Earth. You don't belong here!" Eve continues.

"Eve, or whoever the hell you are, you have to leave. I don't want to entertain your lies anymore. I have no idea what you're talking about." Eight says, as she tries to close the door. Eve stops her before she is able to do so.

Eve's face is now streaming with tears. Strangely enough, her chip does not beep. Only Eight's chip is beeping. Could Eve be telling the truth? Could it be that she doesn't have the chip?

"Ok, fine. I'm leaving. But, if you ever decide to believe me, which I trust you will in time, please call this number." After saying these words, Eve thrusts a piece of paper into Eight's hand and walks away.

Before Eight could close the door, Eve had wandered off. It almost felt as if she was never here.

Extremely confused by the whole ordeal, Eight locks her apartment door and sits down on her sofa. She hides the piece of paper that Eve had given her inside her dress pocket. Eight continues to ponder on the sensation that she had felt with Eve.

It was not like one that she had ever felt before. It felt different, but exciting. Eight felt separated from her very own mind. It was as if her body recognized who Eve is, but her mind had no recollection.

Ten comes home later that night, and Eight tells him what had happened with Eve. Ten refuses to pay attention to anything Eight has to say after she told him that some girl Ten had tried to prostitute off came to their apartment. He becomes frustrated that he had spent all that time kidnapping Fourteen, just to have her escape from the grasp of Zero. He has to find her or else Zero will take away his investment!

Later that night, after Eight had fallen asleep, Ten crawls out of bed and fumbles through her belongings for any clues as to where Fourteen might be. He had watched her apartment all day but did not see her go home.

Then the phone rings, and it is Zero. Zero tells Ten that he no longer wants Fourteen for his prostitution business, or any woman for that matter, and instead schedules a meeting with Ten to discuss other options.

The next afternoon, Ten finds himself back behind the wooden desk at the musty old cabin of Governor Zero. Zero is fiddling with his tie, as usual, as he speaks.

"Well, Ten, you're not very experienced in the business of trafficking, now are you?"

"No sir, and I'm very sorry." Ten replies.

"After that whole fiasco, I don't want you to traffic any more girls for me. I was almost left for dead with her, and I don't need a repeat of that. However, I have another proposal for you." Zero continues.

"And what's that?"

"Do you know that jewelry store downtown called "The Glam"? It is run by one of my greatest business rivals, who is currently doing better than I am. The shop has an expensive diamond necklace on display, one that is worth half their wealth. Of course, I could just buy it if I wanted to, but why would I want to spend my time and money on that when I can just steal it, right, Ten?"

Ten realizes where this conversation is going. Stealing? That is something he has never done before. Plenty of people did it, but Ten had never been bothered to try it. He found no thrill in it. His heart had only ever been thirsty for bloodshed.

"I need you to steal it for me, Ten. Steal it for me, and I'll invest in your business." Zero demands.

Ten contemplates on it for a minute. Even if stealing is something he has never done before, there is a first for everything. Plus, his business is still his highest priority.

Stealing is something he could easily do if it means his business will thrive, that is, if he plans it out right.

Ten nods in agreement to Zero, and both of them shake hands. Ten then leaves the cabin and begins to plot a fool proof plan to steal the necklace.

CHAPTER 10

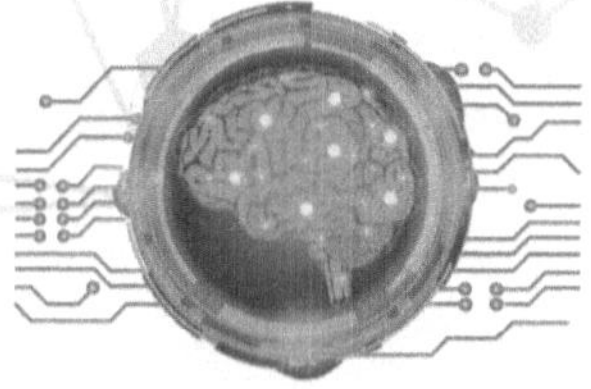

AFTER THAT DAY, Eight had not heard from Eve again. However, Eight still could not get her out of her mind. She sees the outline of Eve's face in her morning coffee, in her mirror as she brushes her hair, and even in her favorite television shows. Sometimes, Eight finds herself staring out the window and seeing Eve's face on the people who walk by.

Eight also continues to have visions of her and Eve, similar to the one she had when Eve showed up days before.

In one of them, she sees herself and Eve drinking coffee at a café that she does not recognize. The café is located outdoors and in the midst of a busy street where everybody has replaced their smiles with frowns toward each other.

Eight sees men and women wearing the most outrageous clothing, different colors and different styles, walking up and down the streets. Both Eight and Eve are laughing and wearing clothes that do not match each other.

Eve is wearing a pink floral dress that reaches down to her knees while Eight is wearing a leather jacket over a white tank top. Everyone looks different. No two people look the same, and Eight can see and hear herself whispering to Eve about how she wishes that she looks like the supermodel on the magazine in front of her.

In another vision, she and Eve are crouching over a mahogany desk, going through some papers that are scattered throughout a welcoming room. They are both wearing the same outfits they had worn in the previous vision.

The whole room is filled with many other desks, over which many other heads are crouching over, with as many men as there are women. Eve whispers something into Eight's ear as her mouth drops open with a gasp when a loud and booming voice interrupts them.

"Densen!" It booms.

The women look, with shocked faces, toward the side of the room the voice had come from.

Suddenly, the vision goes away, and Eight finds herself back on her sofa.

Eight wonders if she should talk to someone, at least a doctor, about the visions that she is having. After all, visions are not normal, right?

However, even doctors would think she's some psycho lunatic if she told them, since being different is not allowed. She would also have to explain to them the constant beeping of her chip, which she is not willing to share with anyone, not even Ten. She knows that if she even mentions her chip, she would instantly become a social outcast and be killed.

Then another vision appears. Eight is sitting behind a small desk, with stacks of books and papers scattered in front of her. Behind her is a tall shelf that towers over her, filled with books upon books on topics related to the psychological mind.

Above her, Eight could see a large banner that read:

"Professor Charlotte Densen on her new book, 'Mind Over Morals'."

In front of her sits a massive crowd of people, both young and old, all dressed in different clothing with different facial expressions, some eager to see her, others arguing with each other, while most bored and staring off into space.

Through the sea of faces, Eight spots a familiar one, Eve, who smiles at her from the front row while holding a sign that reads, "You can do it!" Then Eight hears herself speak:

"Welcome to my book reading. Today, I'm going to read to you a segment from my new book, 'Mind Over Morals'. Thank you for coming, everyone." She says.

She picks up one of the books, which has an image of the brain on the cover, opens it, and clears her throat. Then, she starts reading from it out loud.

"We limit our own freedom. We limit our own free will. How? With a little thing we have come to subconsciously possess, a little thing we like to call 'morals'.

We limit the potential and voice we are capable of by relying on morality. We decide what is right versus what is wrong. We decide who should be punished and who should be rewarded based on our own biased desires and preferences. We create rules that limit some while bringing others to their fruition.

What is morality? Here, I quote an article called the 'Psychology of Morality'. 'Moral principles indicate what is a 'good', 'virtuous', 'just', 'right', or 'ethical' way for humans to behave. Moral rules—and sanctions for those who transgress them—are used by individuals living together in social communities, for instance, to make them refrain from selfish behaviors and to prevent them from lying, cheating, or stealing from others.'

The role of morality is the maintenance of social order, focusing on the display of fairness, empathy, and altruism in face-to-face groups, where individuals all know and depend on each other for survival.

In an analysis provided by Tomasello and Vaish in 2013, this is considered the 'first tier' of morality, where individuals can observe and reciprocate the actions they receive from others, and in turn, elicit and reward cooperative and empathic behaviors that help to protect individual and group survival.

However, there are also abstract moral principles that can be used to regulate and govern the interactions of individuals in more complex societies. This emphasizes more ambiguous concepts such as 'the greater good', leading into what Tomasello and Vaish considered the 'second tier' of morality.

At this level, behavioral guidelines that have lost their immediate survival value in modern societies (such as specific dress codes or dietary restrictions) are seen as essential behaviors that are morally 'right'.

Moral judgments that function to maintain social order in this way rely on behavioral guidelines that were not once seen as important for maintaining order and survival, requiring complex interpretations of moral values and biased judgments.

So, how do we, as a society, deem what is morally right and what is morally wrong? Are we even authorized to determine what morality encompasses based on our own natural discriminations? According to Skitka and Mullen, moral convictions are seen as compelling mandates, indicating what everyone 'ought' to or 'should' do.

People are expected to follow these mandates and are emotionally affected and distressed when they don't, and sometimes resort to violence when the values of others do not align with their own. We go back and forth with what we believe should be mandated rules because we want to be able to benefit ourselves and our social groups while casting aside all others. We constantly change our values on what we believe to be important so we can best protect ourselves, even when our actions go against our previous beliefs.

We live in a society where everyone feels obligated to follow social order, with those at the top having more power and control over their behaviors, as well as a stronger voice in altering the concepts of morality at their own discretion, while those at the bottom are more chastised for rebelling against morality and their own social classes. We become envious when we are placed at the bottom of the social chain and are deemed as outcasts.

Those at the bottom are more limited to freedom than those at the top, more limited to what they can or cannot wear, more limited to what they can or cannot say, and more limited to what they can or cannot do.

They resort to rebellion when the values of their free will are shut down by the values of the socially constructed society, creating chaos in the modern world.

However, what if this is no longer the case? What if the rules of social order no longer exist? What if those at the bottom become just like those at the top? What if the world no longer had discriminations and discrepancies?"

Eight stops speaking, and the vision disappears.

Eight is particularly disturbed by this specific vision because of how detailed it was. Her head throbs and aches from it. She goes to bed, despite it still being early, and doesn't bother making dinner for Ten, afraid of how he would react when he found out. Luckily, he does not come home that night.

He has been spending the past few weeks with the new neighbor who just moved into their building while her husband is off on a business trip. She has been constantly messaging Ten about how lonely she feels during the nights when Ten is in bed with Eight, causing Ten to walk out on Eight and straight upstairs.

Over the next few days, Eight does not experience anymore disturbances or visions. The chip had stopped beeping, and she believes that her life is finally getting back to normal. She goes to The Glam and buys herself a new pair of earrings, snapping over thirty selfies of herself in the process.

She spends half her days sleeping with everyone in the local strip club while half her nights drinking and drinking until she could no longer see, believing that shutting off her vision would prevent her visions.

However, then it all returns.

One late afternoon while Eight is washing the dishes from dinner the previous night, she feels another vision blur her eyesight. She quickly sits down on one of the dining table chairs to prevent herself from crumbling onto the ground. She then whirls into another dream like trance, similar to all the ones before.

This time, Eight finds herself having a vision of a chaotic time she is strangely familiar with. The audio begins playing, as she views herself sitting on a strangely colored couch, with the words "I am Charlotte" written across her forehead.

"It has been over 489 days since the outbreak of the mass suicides began, with its first occurrence in Reykjavík, which resulted in over 8,000 deaths, and is continuing to spread like rapid wildfire across several other continents. The death toll is now up to over 100 billion, and it doesn't look like there is an end in sight!

Day after day, citizens of the world are killing themselves due to high insecurity and the pressure of needing to belong. Everywhere we look, people are different from one another. They look different. They behave different. They even speak different! Normal, right? We're human! We're supposed to be different from one another!

Apparently, not!

Unfortunately, little did I personally know, the entire world is filled with normopaths, constantly craving for acceptance and the chance to be like everyone else, and when they don't succeed, bam! They blow up their own brains!

These normopaths cannot handle the pressure that comes with the reality of life, so therefore, the weak continues to off themselves because they fail to match up to the high pressures of social media that literally brainwash them into believing that they HAVE TO BE THE SAME AS EVERYONE ELSE or else their lives are not worth living! Crazy!"

Charlottes grabs the remote control off the wooden coffee table and turns off the news. She had seen enough.

"UGH!!!!" Charlotte grunts, her head burying in between her knees.

"THIS NEEDS TO END! I'm the best scientist in the world! I won over a dozen awards for my work on the human brain! How can I not figure out how to end this madness! I have to end this! I have to do something to stop this!" She screams out loud.

"People are killing themselves by the second just because they are too insecure to have a little confidence in themselves and not listen to the horrid stories of social media, and it's not necessarily their fault! Insecurity doesn't always stem from the weakness and fragility of the mind; sometimes we become insecure because that's how we were raised. Also, who gives social media the right to tell us how we should be living, and that if we don't live the way that they suggest, then our lives are meaningless!? Bullshit!"

"Honey, are you okay? I heard yelling from inside the kitchen." Charlotte turns around and Eight sees an unfamiliar man standing by the kitchen door, holding a spatula from preparing a dinner of roast beef and tomato pasta.

"Yea, sorry, babe. It's the news." Charlotte replies. "It just got to me. It always gets to me. I need some fresh air. I'll be right back."

"Alright, but be careful out there! People these days do not know what they want. I almost got my arm bit off and returned to me on my way home from the grocery store earlier!"

Frustrated and stressed out, Charlotte walks out of her home and heads off toward the direction of the bridge, mumbling to herself and fidgeting with her fingers as she continues to walk straight. On her way there, she encounters more suicides in person than she had just seen on TV moments ago.

"Jesus, this is really getting out of control." Charlotte whispers to herself.

Over on her left, she sees five cars speeding toward each other and colliding, with all eight people flying out through their windshields and onto the hoods of the opposing car seconds after. Over on her right, she sees people shooting themselves in the heads after reading comments from trolls on social media and losing followers.

Behind her, she can hear more guns firing and ambulances whirling as they are unable to get to the injured because of the chaos that the town has created.

Charlotte then feels her pocket vibrate. Someone had commented on her latest social media post, where she posted a picture of her and her friends celebrating her birthday at a café. The newest comment says, "Charlotte, maybe you should hit the gym instead of the bakery! I think you're done stocking up on rolls."

Her heart and stomach sank. Charlotte's weight was always her biggest source of insecurity. She always fears that with enough comments like these, she may one day end up killing herself also.

"How could people be so cruel? Why can't it just be okay

that I don't look like a supermodel in every photo? Why can't it just be okay that I don't look like a supermodel at all?" Charlotte groans in anger and frustration.

Still, despite her opinionated thoughts and strong feminism, her insecurity continues to creep through. She covers her abdomen with her long cardigan and continues walking. She watches as more and more people jump off the bridge as she crosses it.

She used to intervene when she sees jumpers. She used to try and talk them down, and a fraction of the time, she was successful. However, now it has gotten to the point where there are too many of them to control, and it's better to just leave it.

Charlotte continues to walk until she sees a petite lavender colored home.

"I still can't believe she went with that ugly color. How could she not care what people think of her?" Charlotte says to herself.

She knocks on the door. A woman opens it and smiles.

"Eve, we need to talk." Charlotte demands, as she shuts the purple door behind her.

CHAPTER 11

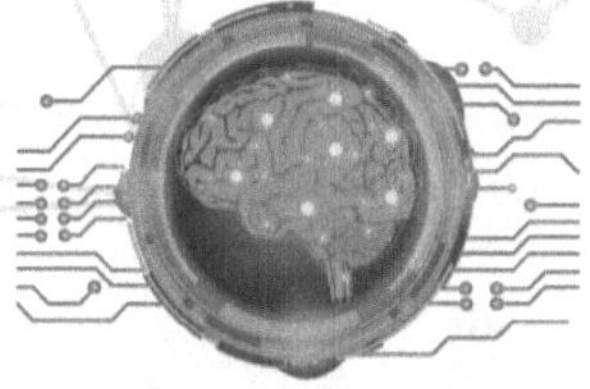

WEEKS HAD PASSED BY, without any news from Eight. Eve did not expect Eight to suddenly believe her and reach out to her, but somewhere in her heart, she had hoped that she would.

Over the past few weeks, Eve had isolated herself inside a small cottage on the outskirts of town to avoid being found. With Nine dead and the assumption that Ten is still on the hunt for her, she no longer feels safe in her own home. She does not trust the people of this society; lying is in their blood.

Eve had stumbled upon this old cottage a few years back,

expecting that one day she would need it if her life is ever in danger.

Eve knows in her heart that the only hope to save the people of Lustville is to revive the creator of the chip, Eight, to get her to reverse the effects, and the only way to do that is to kidnap Eight and force her to remember, force her to remember why she began the invention, force her to remember the research she began working on to stop it.

One gloomy morning, Eve, with the help of a professional kidnapper, sneak into Eight's apartment, drug, and blindfold her as she comes out from the shower. They then load Eight onto the back seat of Eve's car and drive her off to an abandoned building with an office where Eve has been stashing all of Eight's old research.

Eve parks her car across the street from The Glam, places Eight's arm over her shoulder, and drags her into the building and up a dusty and crooked staircase. She hears sirens blaring, cameras clicking, and people applauding behind her but does not care enough to turn her head around to see what's going on.

Eve opens the door of the office and leads Eight inside. With her eyes now slightly open, Eight sees a room with boxes upon boxes of old documents scattered across the floor.

Fearful that Eight might escape, Eve quickly locks the door and shoves the key into her bra. She pushes Eight into the seat behind the desk, rummages through one of the boxes, and takes out a pink folder filled with papers.

"Here, read this." Eve says, as she tosses the folder in front of Eight.

Eight opens the folder and finds an article she had presented eight years ago on the concept of "Normopathy," titled "Who Are You Really?" She picks it up and begins reading.

Have you ever wanted to be like someone else, where the need becomes so strong that you continue to obsess over that desire, refusing to stop until you have achieved that goal? Have you ever despised the body you are in because it doesn't 'align' with the common body type of those around you? Have you ever pursued to belong and pursued for acceptance so intensely that you lose yourself in the process?

'Normopathy' refers to when an individual person, or a group of people, strive to conform and be accepted by the greater society, even if it means risking the loss of their own individualities. Normopathy can also refer to the desire to relinquish individuality because it creates a sense of 'difference' and 'not belonging'.

During the 1970s, a psychoanalyst, Christopher Bollas, termed the phrase 'normotic illness', where people resort to mental breakdowns and violence in response to not fitting in. People who suffer from normotic illness fear loneliness. They always feel the need to belong and yearn for social approval.

'Normopaths', as they are called, lack their own opinions and thoughts. They refuse to act or speak unless they are told to or unless they are certain that their thoughts and opinions will align with that of others. They constantly fear rejection so they look to others on how to behave. These people form their likes and dislikes based on popular opinions, never wearing an outfit before someone else has worn it first and never reading a book before someone else has read it first.

People with normopathy have developed this 'illness' as a source of security. They have had traumatic pasts, either in childhood or young adulthood, where their voices and beliefs have been constantly met with dissatisfaction, criticism, and anger. They have been constantly told they are 'wrong' or that they exist to create chaos and havoc rather than exist for the greater good of humanity.

These people are usually timid and shy, refusing to speak up in crowds except for when they have been addressed directly, and even so, only speak up in agreement. They are met with extreme guilt and shame when they find out that they have disagreed with the larger crowd, only fueling their silences that much more.

Normopaths no longer know why they feel certain ways, only

knowing that they should because everyone else seems to. They no longer behave as functional human beings. Rather, they begin to exist as objects that simply agree and nothing else. They feel empty, unable to generate self-acceptance so they seek external validation.

Every day, we are surrounded by normopaths, unable to tease them out from the crowd because they are experts at fitting in. Our minds are trained to identify and perceive the outspoken and loud as 'being different' rather than those who go unnoticed. Normopaths are the people who want to be like us, as well as the people we want around us, creating a double-edge sword.

CHAPTER 12

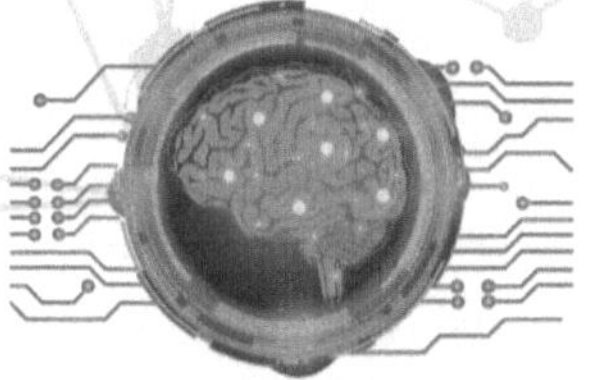

EIGHT STOPS READING midway through the article, lights a match, and burns the papers. She cannot believe the useless and manipulative knowledge that lied inside that article.

'An obsession to be like everyone else? Preposterous!' Eight thinks to herself.

As someone who has become increasingly popular and famous for her writings on individualism and self-acceptance, she refuses to believe that there are people who would want anything but that.

Eve kept Eight locked in the room for many days on end. Throughout these days, all Eight is able to do is read and read piles of articles. She does not attempt to escape, even though she is much stronger than Eve and can if she wants to. She finds herself drawn into her readings, and slowly by slowly, she begins to remember her past.

Eve gradually begins to fill Eight in on what had happened. Eight learns that she had created the chip with the intention of solving the psychological issues of the emotionally vulnerable, to prevent further suicidal behaviors, and to attempt to give people their sense of free will back.

She had intended to make the weak stronger and to devoid the rich and powerful of their excuses to dehumanize the lower class. She had intended to also solve the chaos caused by the clashing of opinions.

Eight remembers now how people argued and fought due to differences of opinions and beliefs between social groups.

In attempts to resolve this, she created a chip that causes everyone's brain and consciousness to become EXACTLY the same, to remove the modern differences of morality and appearances, to remove conflicting thoughts and opinions, to remove the social order and make the behaviors of everyone the same, to remove the concept of restrictions and limitations and allow everyone to have free reign, to utilize the full potential of individual thoughts and preferences, and to completely remove the consequences associated with going against the moral guidelines constructed by society.

She had intended to cure diseases such as depression and jealousy, that created acts of violence. She wanted to ultimately remove the chaos in the world that had caused people to become suicidal for not measuring up to those at the top of the ladder chain and for not measuring up to the impossible standards of society.

However, her research had been highly subjective and discriminatory when it should have been more objective and factual. She failed to take into account that the mind functions in conjunction with the physical body, unable to alter one without affecting the other.

The chip had been a carefully researched device with great promise and potential but ended up becoming a poor and disastrous invention. It had deprived humans of their humanity and only latched onto the minds of the emotionally weak, turning them into clones of one another with pre-programmed emotions, engaging in behaviors without understanding the consequences, instead of emotionally strong humans with self-acceptance and self-love.

It created a society of murderers, liars, cheaters, and all things sin rather than a society of equality and social justice.

As Eight learns more about the chip, she no longer feels trapped and confused. She now begins to understand the reason for her apathy and self-destructive behaviors, and why she had felt conflicting thoughts but had no control over them.

The more Eight recollects her studies and work, the more determined and engaged she becomes in continuing her research on how to undo the apocalypse created by the chip. She finds herself becoming more emotional to her memories of murdering and cheating as she learns to become more human.

However, as Eight's emotions become more developed, she suddenly finds herself becoming more depressed. She finds herself becoming more disappointed over issues she would not have normally been disappointed over, such as her husband's disregard for her absence, and his continual infidelity, actions she believes are results of the brainwashing. Ten has not called Eight once, but instead, had posted about his newest affair on BLykeMe.

Eight's visions do not stop, but they make much more sense to her now. She soon begins remembering bits and pieces of her old life, such as how she likes to eat bacon and eggs for breakfast rather than plain rice cakes, how she used to be loyal and devoted to her boyfriend who still lives back on Earth, how the thought of infidelity and being with Ten disgusts her, and how she used to be a strong and independent woman, with an outspoken mind, rather than a submissive whore.

Eight then finds a video, a DVD of a recording from when she presented her research on the chip at an annual scientific conference in Osaka. She inserts it into the outdated DVD player beside her and begins watching.

"The human mind is very complex. It is both intellectual, yet dysfunctional, and when steered in the wrong direction, it can wreak havoc on society. The social order of society has taken away the human right to choose and belong, forcing us to fight for what is ours and fight for our place in this world, putting a dent in the structure of order and as a result, creating even more destruction, and sometimes even death.

Look around you. Everyone wishes they could be someone else. The wealthy wishes to achieve more humility and compassion. The humble wishes to achieve more materialism and success. Not one single person around you is satisfied with his or her life.

People wish that they can be the person on their right or the person on their left, creating a mindset of social dysfunction and depression. Over the past sixteen months, nearly 100 billion people have committed suicide because they wished to be different, to be someone they were not, and when they did not fulfill that need to fruition, they lost hope in living.

You are sitting in this auditorium today because you wish you could also be different. You wish you could be the person sitting next to you, be the person who fits in with society, and be the person who no longer have to follow the social order of structure. You are tired of the constant limitations that confine you to your part of the world, unable to interact with those from other parts, and unable to enact in the behaviors and mindsets that those in other groups are able to.

Well, ladies and gentlemen, you no longer have to live in a world of anger and envy. You no longer have to live in a mindset where you constantly yearn to be someone else or constantly yearn to be able to engage in the activities and behaviors of those in other social groups. You no longer have to utter the words 'That's not fair' to yourself.

I present to you 'Separvoc', the first genetically designed microchip that grants your wishes to become just like everyone else. No longer will you have to live in the anxiety and envy of being different. No longer will you have to scroll through the social media pages of influencers and wish you are them instead of yourself. No longer will you have to be an outcast in a world where the upper class have different rules than the lower. No longer will you have to subject yourself to restrictions, where you are unable to express your own voice and opinions.

With Separvoc, everyone becomes the same, everyone is given equal chance to speak and behave as they wish without the rules of the social order imposed on them. Envy will cease to exist because differences will become a thing of the past.

Imagine a world that is a complete replicate of the one you have always dreamt of, a world where you are free to express your emotions and desires without the morals of society limiting you to certain actions and phrases. A world where the concept of free will can truly exist. Imagine a world where anything and everything you want become reality, a world where violence and suicide have vanished, a world where everyone can be satisfied and happy.

Separvoc detaches your mind from your body, allowing you to behave without the constant thoughts and worries of guilt and shame that would otherwise prevent you. Your mind no longer prevents the desires of your body from coming to life. Your mind is no longer controlled and limited from expressing the life your body wants to express.

Separvoc is designed to attach to your brain, making you believe that morals no longer have to be followed and differences are no longer a part of reality. Separvoc is the invention of the future, where everyone becomes one, and no one will ever need to suffer again."

CHAPTER 13

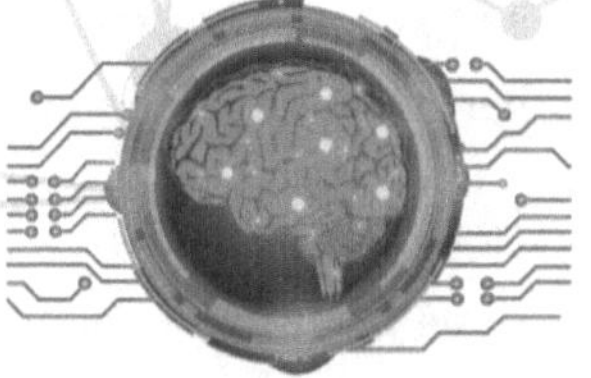

EIGHT FINDS herself growing increasingly depressed and conflicted over the next few days, as she battles between the powers of the chip and her own personal instincts. The chip in her head beeps louder and louder the more Eight learns about her past and tries to deactivate Separvoc.

The more she learns about the new world she has created, the more increasingly aware she becomes of the people around her. She begins to notice how similar everyone is and how robotic everyone has become.

Everywhere she turns, people are walking down the

streets, with simultaneous steps one by one, smiling endlessly without reason on blank faces, and posting updates and photos on their phones regardless of where they are.

Everyone around Eight looks exactly the same, the only difference being the gender. Men and women both have silver white locks on their heads while adorning their bodies with silver garments and black shoes.

However, the strangest part is, no one seems to notice. The people do not seem to be aware of the fact that they look exactly like the people walking on either side of them. The people of Lustville do not seem to be aware that they post their outfits on BLykeMe, thinking they stand out, when only one outfit exists in the entire town.

The chip makes Eight want to conform to the heinous rules that her current society follows.

It wants her to shut down her feelings and morals. Although Eight could have done that previously, her learned knowledge causes her to feel extreme guilt for creating the apocalypse that destroyed society and resulted in the deaths of so many people when she was only trying to save them.

The final straw came one afternoon. Tired with her reading, her mind saturated and foggy, Eight walks down the street to grab a cup of coffee from the local café. On her way there, she hears a woman scream loudly behind her. She turns around and sees a young girl being stabbed multiple times by an older man after she was mugged and raped.

Eight watches as the girl bleeds to her death on the hood of a rusty car while everyone, even the police, around her continues to take pictures, not one single person caring enough to call an ambulance. She then walks over and leans closer. It was Eve. She had been attacked while running out to her car to grab the files that documented how Eight could turn Separvoc off.

. . .

Usually, Eight would not have cared. In fact, she would have joined them in snapping photos, even taking a selfie with the body to boost her social media pages. However, this time, she could not shake what had happened.

Over the course of the past few weeks, she had developed morals and emotions that now cannot be distracted with anything else, not even lust. She had attempted to sleep with every man she saw walk down the streets, but her mind refused to let her proceed past first base as she began to feel guilty for potentially cheating on Ten.

Eight's head throbs, her vision blackens, and she could feel sparks of electricity shooting out from the top of her head. Her entire life begins to flash rapidly through her mind as she experiences her entire timeline, from childhood to when she first became interested in the human mind to her first job to her first relationship, all within seconds.

Separvoc is glitching and malfunctioning because Eight has broken the unspoken rules of having morals and emotions, for caring about the feelings of others, and for experiencing guilt for her actions of free will.

She can no longer bear the pain that her head is causing her. She knows too much to distract her mind and turn the chip off, and she never got the chance to read up on how to deactivate it. Her only option now, is to cut the chip out, to remove it before it causes her to shatter and disintegrate.

The pain increases, and Eight runs like a lunatic through the streets of Lustville, screaming to herself to stop the agony, while everyone in town watches in confusion, distraught, and fear.

Eight makes her way to an isolated river in the secluded forest, takes a knife out from under her long silver dress, flowing in the wind, and makes a deep cut into her right temple, digging her fist into her head, laughing insanely, as she rips out the electrified microchip and drops it in the water.

"I want to be just like everyone else. I want to be just like everyone else. I want to be just like everyone else." Eight says, repeatedly, laughing as she steps into the river, falls back, and flows away with the current, leaving a trail of blood behind.

The entire town of Lustville had gone to the river, hoping to witness and record the downfall of the town's "lunatic." However, rather than taking out their phones, like they used to, one by one, they each pull out their own knives and cut into their own right temples, one by one, reaching their fists inside their heads and pulling out their own individual microchips.

They do not know why, but watching Eight do it compelled them to also do the same. One by one, each person drops their electrified chip onto the muddy ground, stomps on it, and one by one, they each walk into the river, fall back, and wash away with the current, leaving a trail of blood behind in the dark, cold, empty, and silent town of Lustville.

EPILOGUE

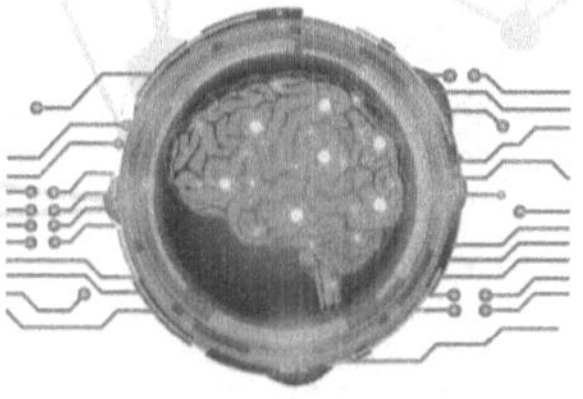

DIFFERENCES in human personality serve as a way for us to express our own individualities and strive to become the people we want to be. We were all born different, all born with different thoughts and opinions on morality and how we should function as part of society.

The social order of society was created to prevent those with mindsets of harming themselves and others from coming to fruition while allowing those with mindsets of achieving the greater good to flourish.

We think we want to be the same as the person next to us.

We think that if we are just richer, prettier, or smarter, then our lives would be better. We look at influencers, celebrities, and supermodels, wishing we have their lives.

But envy is only temporary. We think we know what we want because our current lives are going downhill while it seems like the lives of others are only getting better and better.

However, what we don't realize is that each and every person has their own strengths and weaknesses. Having what everyone else has or being what everyone else is removes our own individualities, causing us to become numb and robotic creatures who blindly act and speak without knowing why.

A world where everyone is the same only welcomes chaos and destruction. We think we cannot be happy with our individual differences, but a world that takes away uniqueness and order only leaves us craving for more.

We are all different for a reason, to share with others what they do not have while receiving what we do not have. Not everyone's appearance represents how they truly feel on the inside. Becoming someone we wish we could be cannot solve our problems.

Being on the opposing end of the social construct doesn't always guarantee satisfaction. Running away from our difficulties is never the answer.

We are most vulnerable to change and ideas when we are emotional. Our emotions are what make us unique, yet they are also what drive us toward change and dissatisfaction. We have the tendency to not disagree with those around us for the fear of becoming social outcasts. We have the tendency to become who and what others want us to be even when we disagree.

Be careful for what you wish for.
You might just get it.

Based on true experiences of the modern world.

www.ingramcontent.com/pod-product-compliance
Lightning Source LLC
Chambersburg PA
CBHW031018190726
48286CB00003BA/911